LICK AND THE INVASION

BOOKS 4 - 6

LICK DARSEY

BRIGHT AURORA MEDIA

ISBN: 978-1-7320606-5-4

DEDICATION_

Me and Fanger are dedicated to whoopin' alien ass in space.

CONTENTS

INTRODUCTION_

Me, Fanger and Jack had a lot of learning to do. And like always, them alien critters kept us on our toes. But we were always ready for a fight.

THE DIVERSION

BOOK 4

RECONNECTED_

THE FIRST THANG we did once it sank in we was drifting in space was to check supplies. We figured we had enough beer and airplane bottles of whiskey for a good week and a half and we could run the moonshine still off and on to get us through to four weeks. That left us about a month to either get back to Earth or find some space beverages. Other shit like food and water we could figure out along the way.

Jack spent all his time in the big ass lounge chair, tinkering with the controls and trying to learn the ins and outs of the ship. Since he figured out how to control them clones, he was able to put them sumbitches to work cleaning up the mess we left from the battle.

Me and Fanger did a little exploring but never

found any thang useful. We farted on the walls, passed through the Jell-O and ended up in some empty ass room. We never went more than three rooms past the control room. We still weren't sure what made the ship transform and didn't want to risk getting isolated from Jack or the supplies. Eventually we unpacked our camping chairs, drank moderately to ration alcohol, breathed in the fresh ass air and tried to remember any thang we could about the whoop ass device.

"I figure it ain't in the junkyard," Fanger said, staring up at the ceiling.

"Why is that?" I asked, doing the same damn thang.

"We never hide heavy duty shit at the junkyard anymore. Specially after what happened with the laser canon." Fanger took a deep breath and closed his eyes.

"Yep, we learned our lesson with that shit." I took a deep breath and closed my eyes too.

After several minutes of silence, I titled my head forward, put both hands on the arms of the chair, and pushed myself up to git another beer. Soon as my hands lifted off the chair I damn near passed out. With my eyes closed, I dropped back down in my seat. I took a deep breath and opened my eyes to see the walls swirling like a mixed up rainbow again. "What the hell?" I hollered.

"That's me! I can change the ship!" Jack said from the lounge chair. "Kinda!"

Me and Fanger rocked out of our chairs, keeping our eyes on the floor. When we looked up, the hallway that was leading up to the MTRV was gone. A big room with rounded walls and a shit load of shelves sat where the hallway used to be.

"Look at that shit," Fanger said, leaning his head to the right and looking in to the room.

Jack popped up and hooked his elbows over the arms of the chair. "Let's go check that shit out," he said, kicking his legs over the arm, dropping down to the platform and on to the floor. He took off for the room like a kid going for his presents at Christmas.

Me and Fanger moved in slow and steady, scanning the room with each step. All our gear from the MTRV sat to left of the entrance and a shit ton of black colored square boxes sat on the rows of shelves in the room.

"Weapons?" Fanger said, screwing the lid on his jar of moonshine.

Jack snatched one of the devices off the wall and tossed it around in his hands.

"Careful, Jack!" I hollered.

"It's light as shit," Jack said, grinning from ear to ear.

I clenched my jaw and picked up my pace. Soon as I got to the archway leading into the new room a whizzing sound tingled in my ear. "You doing that, Jack?" I said, glancing over at Fanger.

"Not on purpose." Jack slipped the black box in his right pocket and backed away from the shelves.

The intercom crackled and a voice hollered, "We found you sumbitches!"

"Back to your chair, Jack!" I hollered.

Jack lifted his lanky knees high to his chest, swung his long arms and hauled ass back to the lounge chair. His left foot hit the platform, and with a grunt, he pushed off and twisted around in to the chair.

"We're movin'." Fanger pointed to the TV screen with his pokey fanger and grabbed a beer out of the cooler with his left hand. Colors streaked across the screen and the whizzing sound grew faster and louder.

"Them alien critters reestablished connection! They got control of the ship again!" Jack hollered.

"Hey! Alien critter!" I said, cracking open a beer. "What the hell's goin' on?"

"We're taking our ship back, asshole!" the voice said over the intercom.

"He sounds pissed." Fanger scrunched up his forehead and sipped his beer.

I squeezed my beer tight in my left hand and trotted over to the big ass lounge chair. With a leap, I kicked my right leg up and on to the the platform. Bringing my left foot up next to my right, I stretched my neck and leaned over the arm of the chair to look down at Jack. "Where they takin' us?" I said in low voice.

"Back to Earth is what I reckon," Fanger said, looking over the other arm of the chair.

"Maybe," Jack mumbled, his fangers dancing around on the control panel sitting over the top of his lap.

"Let'em fly us back." I looked up at Fanger and raised my eyebrows. "At least we'll git back to Earth. We can figure out how to whoop their asses once we're back."

Fanger nodded and pulled his head back to sip his beer. "Looky there," he said, shifting his eyes towards the TV screen.

I dropped my heels to the platform, leaned towards the screen and said, "That Earth?"

"Um, uh," Jack tapped away on his control.

I lifted my beer to take sip and damn near fell off the platform. The walls swirled around in different colors again and I got so swimmy headed I dropped my damn beer. I tried to cuss but my jaw locked up, my arms and legs snapped together and the next thang I knew I was floating through the air. As I drifted away from the chair, Jack and Fanger floated up next to me. Both of them was straight as a pencil.

My body rotated slowly and one whole side of the ship opened up in to space. I hovered in one spot for second staring down at the planet below. It looked like pictures I'd seen of Earth from space but the blues and the greens was brighter.

A fizzy sound tickled my ears causing me to close eyes. When I opened them again, some kinda clear bubble surrounded my body. The same whizzing sound I hear when the ship moves buzzed in my ear and I took off in to space. The planet grew closer and closer and before long it looked like shit does when looking out of an airplane. Big ass buildings stuck up towards the sky, all surrounded by bright green and blue. Ships or some shit zipped around below in straight lines like they was following some kinda traffic pattern. I was moving so fast I couldn't git a good look at any of it.

After a few seconds, I slowed down and a

building centered in my line of sight. It was a tall grayish black skyscraper type building poking up like a spike outa the greenest bunch of grass and trees I'd ever seen. I leveled off with the top of the spike and the bubble shot me straight for the building. Soon as I was about to hit the outside wall, a little hole opened up and I flew right through it.

I hovered in the middle of the room, still unable to move shit, and saw Jack and Fanger float up next to me out of the corner of my eye. A swoosh fluttered in my ear and the bubble was gone. My body floated for another second and I sank to floor, real slow and steady. When my feet hit the ground, I bounced my knees and shook out my arms, not really sure when I got my movement back.

"You fellers a'ight?" I said, turning my head between Fanger on my right and Jack on my left.

"Yep." Fanger twisted his head around, checking out the room we landed in.

"Shit if I know," Jack said, crossing his arms and turning slowly.

I rotated on my right heel and scoped shit out. The room was a big ass rectangle about the size of a double wide trailer with grayish black walls and a ceiling that was high as hell. There weren't shit in the room but the three of us. I inhaled deep and took in the air. It was even fresher than the air on the space ship.

Next thang I knew a door opened in the wall and a space hillbilly feller stood in the door way. He looked kinda like the one Fanger caught with same blue skin but his green hair and beard were brushed out and he looked a lot stronger than the other critter. He hooked his thumbs through his red overall straps, no clothes underneath on this feller either, and just stared at us for a couple seconds.

"You sumbitches have a choice" he said, not walking all the way in to the room. "Give us the whoop ass device and we'll let y'all live in The Tower. If you don't y'all are goin' to The Hole."

I looked over at Fanger and Jack. The smiles dropped of their faces and their eyebrows scrunched up just like mine.

"Tower?" Jack said.

"Hole?" Fanger said.

That space feller didn't say shit. I stepped towards him and opened up both my hands in front of me. "Listen here, space hillbilly feller, we ain't got no whoop ass—"

Before I could finish, the floor opened up under my feet and I was falling in to pitch black darkness. I flapped my arms and kicked my legs, fighting to get control of my body. My stomach fluttered faster as I gained speed, and I pulled my knees in and flexed my abs while swanging my arms in wide circles, struggling to keep from launching in to a full spin. Just as I caught my balance I thumped down on something kinda soft and the wind huffed out of me. Fanger and Jack thudded right down next to me, heaving from the impact.

I laid there on my back taking in deep breaths, the air was still fresh as hell where ever we was, and looked straight up in to the darkness above. Without moving my body, I shifted my eyes to the right and saw Fanger laying still as shit. I looked to my left and Jack was in the same position as me and Fanger.

"Dirt," Jack said, lifting his right arm and letting dirt fall through his fangers.

I slid my hands down by my hips, patted the the soft ground around me and squeezed my fist. My hands filled up with cool, soft dirt. "You fellers a'ight?" I said, still not moving.

"Yep," Fanger and Jack said at the same time.

I lifted my head and looked over the top of Fanger. Dirt walls with roots and shit poking through was ever where. I turned my neck and peered over the top of Jack. A small tunnel just wide enough to walk through single file stretched out in to the dirt.

I kicked my feet and rolled up to a seated position with knees bent and my hands still on the ground by my hips. Swiveling my head all around, I sensed something was weird but I couldn't put my fanger on it.

"Dirt's glowin'," Fanger said, rolling over on to his hands and knees.

Fanger was damn sure right. Ever bit of dirt had a glow to it. I rocked back, rolled up to my feet and said, "That sumbitch called this The Hole."

Fanger jumped his feet up between his hands and straightened up, feeling in his pocket for an airplane bottle of whiskey. "Dammit," he mumbled, pulling his hand from his pocket and glancing around at the dirt room. "Sure as hell looks like a hole."

"Hold up," Jack said, standing up and brushing the dirt off his pants, "Y'all hear that shit?"

Fanger nodded and pointed at the dirt wall behind me with his pokey fanger.

I turned my ear towards the wall and listened. "Sounds like diggin'."

I rotated around to follow the noise and Fanger and Jack moved in next to me. I stepped real slow, my feet sinking in to the soft dirt, and scanned the wall in front of me. Dirt fell off the wall about three feet up from the ground and tiny hole appeared. As the digging sound sped up, dirt fell faster from the wall and the hole grew bigger and bigger.

I slapped my right hip with my right hand, wrapping my fangers around my pistol. I didn't give a shit if the bullets didn't work on these space sumbitches. I always had my pistol on my side. I raised my left hand, took one step closer and closed my fist.

Me, Fanger and Jack stood side by side, Fanger with his hand on his hip too, watching the hole in the wall get bigger. The digging sound stopped and a second later the top of a hat poked through the hole.

"Git ready," I said, keeping my eyes locked on the hole and tightening my grip on my pistol.

The hat, which was so dirty I didn't have a damn clue what color it was, pushed through the hole and turned upwards. A set of green eyeballs peered up at us followed by the dirty face of one of them space hillbillies. Clumps of dirt dangled from the critters face and that sumbitch just starred at us for a couple seconds. "You the new fellers?" he said, shifting his eyes between the three of us.

I looked to my left at Fanger and to my right at Jack, not really sure what the hell to say. We all straightened up and took a few steps back.

The space hillbilly feller squeezed his hands up

beside his head, stretched his arms out of the hole and spread them out along the dirt wall. With a wiggle, he pulled himself through to hole, somehow getting his right leg out before he dropped to the ground.

"Who the hell are you?" I said.

"I'm a prisoner just like you fellers." The dirty critter dusted himself off with his hat even though it didn't do a damn bit of good.

"Prisoners? This is a prison?" Jack said.

"Yep. The Hole is a prison. You fellers dumb or sumpin'?" The space hillbilly ran his tongue around the inside of his left check.

Fanger dropped his arms by his side, leaned forward and stepped for that sumbitch.

"Hold up, Fanger." Jack turned and stretched his lanky left arm across Fanger's shoulders.

I expected Fanger to pop Jack in jaw and move on to whopping that space critters ass but he stopped. "A'ight," Fanger said with a spit.

"We ain't dumb," Jack said, letting his arm drop away from Fanger. "We just ain't from this here planet. We don't know what the hell is goin' on."

The space hillbilly looked around, slapped his hat on his head and turned back to his tunnel in the wall. He bent over, stretched out his arms like he was gonna dive in a swimming pool and then stood up straight again. Spinning around real fast he said, "Maybe we can work together fellers."

"How's that?" I said.

The dirty space hillbilly darted his eyes around, looked over his left shoulder and said, "Escape."

I frowned a little and looked over at Jack. He bounced his right shoulder and shook his head. I turned to Fanger and he stood there with his arms down by his side and jaw clenched like he was still ready whoop that fellers ass.

"You don't even know us," I said. "What makes you wanna help us escape."

The space feller chuckled and snatched his hat off his head. "I ain't helpin' you boys. I need y'all to help me."

"What hell does that mean?" I said.

"Means none of the other prisoners will help me escape." The dirty sumbitch stood there bunching his hat up in his fist like he was pissed off or something. "I figured I might as well ask you fellers."

I stuck my arms out, grabbed Fanger and Jack by the shoulders and pulled them in for a huddle. "What do y'all reckon?" I said in low voice.

"What do we got to lose?' Jack said, digging in

the dirt with his right foot. "What the hell else we gonna down here?"

"Fanger?" I said, looking back to see if that critter was still there.

"I don't give a shit." Fanger spit in the middle of the huddle. "If he tricks us or some shit he's dead."

"A'ight." I let go of Fanger and Jack's shoulders and turned around."Let's git the hell outa here."

The space hillbilly feller grinned, showing the dirt all caked up in his teeth.

"I'm Lick. This here's Fanger and this here's Jack. What's your name?"

The alien critter slapped his hat on his head and said, "Peen-Iz."

"Huh, huh, huh," I chuckled. "Say that again."

"Peen-Iz. Name's Peen-Iz."

"Ha, ha, ha!" Me, Fanger and Jack all laughed our asses off.

"Your name," Fanger said wiping tears off his cheek, "your name is Penis?"

"Yeah, Peen-Iz. What the hell is funny about that shit?" Peen-Iz crossed his arms and turned his head to the side.

"His name is Penis!" I said loud as hell. I grabbed my sides and bent over, looking to my right at Fanger.

"Penis!" Fanger said with his eyes closed. "That's even better than an ass whoopin'!"

"Hey Penis," Jack said, "Can you point us outa here?

We laughed our asses off for so long I lost track of time. Peen-Iz just stood there watching, trying to figure out what the hell was so funny. Eventually I got my shit together. "Penis, do you have an escape plan or what?"

"Hell yeah," Peen-Iz said. "A damn good good one. I can git us off the whole damn planet."

Me, Fanger and Jack all gave him a nod, fighting hard as hell not to laugh. For the time being Peen-Iz was our best bet out of The Hole.

THE HOLE_

ME, Fanger and Jack follered Peen-Iz through one tunnel after the other. That little feller could bore through dirt like a mole or some shit. Some tunnels were big and open and others were so tight we had to crawl through one at a time. We proceeded with caution, not really sure how much we could trust him, but at the same time not having any other options. As we moved through the tunnels, we caught glimpses of all kinda alien critters but we never did git a good look at any of them sumbitches. According to Peen-Iz, they was all squeamish of new arrivals. All except him. He liked meeting the new prisoners.

Not only was Peen-Iz one hell of a tunnel digger, he was talky as shit. His mouth didn't stop moving for a second, pointing out the alien critters that dispersed as they saw us approaching and explaining in almost too much detail how The Hole worked. Basically, The Hole was a buncha dirt and roots in a big ass bubble. The bubble served as a force field keeping all the prisoners from digging out. And from what I understood, Peen-Iz talked so fast and jumped from subject to subject it was hard to keep up, the dirt glowed for a purty simple reason. To give the prisoners light.

In between the alien critter sightings and useless facts about dirt and tunnel digging, Peen-Iz sprinkled in a few comments here and there about escape. Apparently there were only two options to liberate ourselves from The Hole. One was to climb up the way we dropped in. That was purty much impossible. And despite the nonstop chatter, Peen-Iz was still working his way around to telling us the second option.

"Y'all see that shit?" Peen-Iz said, jogging towards the bend in the tunnel ahead. "That was a caterfeller. Them sumbitches look like a mix between us and a hairy worm. You'd think they'd be good in the The Hole but they can't dig for shit."

"Hey, Penis," I said, cutting him off before he

could launch in to another story, "when you gonna tell us the escape plan?"

"I'm gettin' to it." Peen-Iz pointed down a tunnel and said, "That right there is the room where ya'll dropped in. We're goin' to the supply room which is the next room over. That's where we'll escape from."

"What the hell, Penis?" Jack said, chuckling a little at his name. "Why the hell did you walk us all around if we only had to go to the next room over?"

"I figured y'all wanted to see the place. You know, being from another planet and shit." Peen-Iz stopped in his tracks, turned around and looked at us with his jaw hanging open.

"Stop pissin' around and get to it, Penis," Fanger said, slapping my shoulder with a snort.

Peen-Iz threw his right arm in the air, spun around on his right heel and waved us ahead, running his mouth the whole time. After weaving through a couple bends in the tunnel we stepped in to an archway. A collection of containers sat in the center of the room ahead of us and several alien critters was huddled over the top of them. Soon as they caught a whiff of us they scattered like roaches through little tunnels in the dirt walls.

"Supplies," Peen-Iz said moseying over to the containers. "The bigguns don't want prisoners in

The Hole to die. They wanna keep'em alive and use'em for information."

The bigguns was what Peen-Iz kept calling our captures. That and a buncha dumb, stankin', worthless asshole sumbitches. He said it the same way ever time. A buncha dumb, stankin', worthless asshole sumbitches.

"So Penis," I said with a half smile, "what the hell kinda information do the bigguns want from prisoners anyhow?"

"Information to git shit they want," Peen-Iz said with his back turned. He kept speaking as he pried open a container lid with his dirty fingers. "Ever body in The Hole has information or some shit the bigguns want. Most prisoners don't last too long down here and they break. The Hole gets to people. But not me. Ain't shit that gits to me."

"How long you been here?" I said, watching Peen-Iz pop the lid open and bend over into the container.

"Good while, I reckon." Peen-Iz straightened up and turned around, hugging a buncha packages about the size of little packs of instant grits in his arms. "I ain't like other prisoners. I don't break for shit. Can't nobody git information outa me."

"You sure about that?" Jack said, looking at me and Fanger. "I mean, it might take a while but—"

"I'm not too sure I understand," I said, cutting Jack off before he had a chance to piss Peen-Iz off.

"Y'all really don't know shit, do ya?" Peen-Iz shifted the packages in to his left arm and offered each of us one with his right hand.

We all shook our heads, not sure what the hell he wanted to give us, and stared straight at Peen-Iz.

"This here planet is called Bom'Kyn. I'm Bom'Kynian. We don't invent shit. We steal shit." Peen-Iz ripped open the top of a package, tossed his head back and slurped down whatever the hell was in damn thang. He wiped his mouth and beard with the back of his right hand and noticed me taking in a deep breath.

"Air's fresh as shit ain't it?" he said with smile. "We stole the fresh air technology a long time ago."

"Stole it from who?" Fanger crossed his arms and titled his head to the side, expecting Peen-Iz to get long-winded again.

"Shit if I know. It was long time ago. But we stole sumpin' from damn near ever planet around. That's why ever body wants to kill us." Peen-Iz ripped open another package and slurped it down. "We stole space ship technology. Cloning technology. This her bubble technology was stole. Bom'Kynians ain't never invented nothing on their own. I'll bet they want to steal sumpin' from you fellers too. That's why y'all are down here."

I shifted my eyes between Fanger and Jack. From the looks on their faces they was like me. They wasn't too sure about how much to tell Peen-Iz.

"I'll take that as a yes." Peen-Iz dropped his empty packages, spread his arms wide and waved us back. Once we was standing in the archway he pointed over his shoulder with his right thumb and said, "That's our way out."

A bubbled dropped out of the ceiling and floated down, popping when it hit the ground and depositing a new container of supplies.

"More damn bubbles," Jack said, rubbing his hands together.

"Them supply bubbles pass through the big bubble force field," Peen-Iz said. "As they penetrate the barrier you can belly up next to them and squeeze through to the other side."

"Why can't you do that yourself?" Jack asked, starting to pace back and forth.

"I do. All the time," Peen-Iz sniffed and pulled clumps of dirt outa his beard. "The other side of the forcefield is the supply room. I can git in there but that's as far as I can git."

"Why?" Jack's voice was sounding more anxious.

"Guards," Fanger said, his eyes following Jack as he paced in circle.

"That's right." Peen-Iz pointed at Fanger. "I can't git past them guards on my own. If I try to fight them alone they'll set off the alarm and call in reinforcements. That's why I need more people. We gotta neutralize them guards all at the same time so they can't trigger the alarm."

"You said you got a plan, right?" I put my right hand on Jack's shoulder to stop his pacing around.

"Shit yeah," Peen-Iz said. He walked us through the plan, explaining ever little damn detail. But overall, it was really a simple process. Climb up to the edge of the big ass bubble the makes up The Hole. Breach the forcefield. Take out the guards. Stowaway on a ship. Take over the ship once it was in space. All shit we could handle.

Peen-Iz lead us to the back of the room and tugged on one of the roots sticking out of the dirt. "This shit is solid," he said, not bothering to brush off the dirt that fell on his face as he tugged. "Grip tight and climb. Easy as shit."

I stepped up beside Peen-Iz and extended my

right hand, grabbing hold of one of the roots. The damn thang was about two inches thick and smooth as hell. My eyes follows Peen-Iz as he scampered up the wall fast as shit.

I looked back at Fanger and Jack, lined my hips up with the wall, and with a jump, grabbed on to the root with both hand. I dug my feet in to the dirt wall, twitching my ankles around to get a foot hold, and leaned back to test the shit out. After a few bounces, I pulled up, stretched my left hand high to grab the roots above and stepped up with my right foot. It was a purty damn easy climb.

I followed Peen-Iz as best I could. That sumbitch was up the wall in a flash. Jack fell in behind me and damn near past me on the dirt wall. The combination of his long, lanky arms and legs and his growing nervousness gave him a slight advantage. Fanger brought up the rear, dangling from the roots and making Tarzan noises the whole way to the top.

Just before the wall started to curve and turn in to a ceiling, I wiggled my feet in to the dirt and clung to the roots. Holding my position, I twisted my head around, not sure where Peen-Iz went.

A ladder made from roots tied together dropped out of the ceiling a few feet over from me and Peen-Iz hollered, "Climb that shit!"

I let go with my right hand, stretched my arm back and grabbed on to the ladder. The damn thang was stiff and only had a little swang in it. I rotated my shoulders, let got of the roots with my left hand and let my body fall toward the ladder. Once I had a grip with my left hand, I slid my feet out of the dirt wall and my lower body swang right over the ladder. After bouncing a couple times, I climbed fast as hell up through the dirt. The tunnel was tight but lit good with the glowing dirt. I musta climbed twelve feet before reaching a little cave Peen-Iz had dug out.

"Comin' through!" Jack hollered, punching my shoes with his right fist to nudge me on in to the cave.

I crawled to left, the cave was only about four feet high, and hunkered down by the wall. Jack laid out flat, rolled to right of the entrance and stayed on his side. The room was too small for him to sit up good. Fanger stood on the ladder, poking his head up in to the cave.

Peen-Iz leaned against a fat root at the rear of the cave, reached his right arm back and dug around in the a wall, smiling at us with a shit eating grinning the whole time. He rotated his shoulder and pulled a little box out of the dirt. After a few taps to get the dirt off, he flipped open the lid. Turning the box towards us he said, "We're gonna need these."

Leaning forward, I stretched my neck and looked to see what Peen-Iz had to show us. Four shiny little knives, all with blades about two inches long, rattled around in the bottom of the box.

"Take one," Peen-Iz said, extending his arm. "These here are for cutting the straps on the light suit overalls. That's the only way to deactivate them. Once the suits don't work them sumbitches is a lot more vulnerable."

Me, Fanger and Jack stretched our right arms and each pulled a knife out with our pointer fanger and thumb.

"Do we have to cut both straps or what?" Jack tapped the tip of his blade with his left middle fanger.

"Nah, just one will do. Now, check this out," Peen-Iz extended his hands over his head. He dug his fangers in to the sides of a container lid he had stuck up against the top of the cave. He jiggled the lid, not giving a shit that dirt was dropping down on his face, and let the lid drop back behind his head. With a dirty-toothed grin, he pointed up and said, "Supply room."

The container lid was covering the edge of the forcefield. Once Peen-Iz removed it we could see right up in to the supply room above. "Ho. Lee. Shit," Me, Fanger and Jack said at the same time.

"You're gonna wanna move, Jack," Peen-Iz said.

Fanger stepped down the ladder and I squeezed over to one side of the cave as far as I could. Jack slithered like a snake over the top of the entrance and wiggled his way against the wall next to me. A bubble with a container floating inside dropped down through the dirt just beside the edge of the forcefield Peen-Iz had uncovered, passed right by the spot where Jack had been laying and sank out of the cave.

"I'll go through with the next one." Peen-Iz positioned himself in the center of the cave. "When a bubble pokes through the forcefield you can squeeze up next to it and go through the forcefield too. Soon as you see the bubble poke through, reach your arms up high as shit, jump, grab on to the supply room floor and pull yourself up through the forcefield. You can touch bubbles that got shit inside. Just don't touch an empty bubble once you git in the supply. That shit it'll suck you up and you can't git out."

I looked down at Fanger with my face all scrunched up. "Say that shit again," I said, looking back towards Peen-Iz.

"Here comes one. Just watch this." Peen-Iz did

just like he said. He stretched his arms up high, jumped, grabbed the floor and pulled himself in to the room above. It looked easy enough.

Fanger climbed the ladder and got in to position next, keeping his eyes on the supply room. A bubble dropped down and Fanger did just like Peen-Iz. He was up and in the room easy as shit.

"I'm ready to git the shit outa here," Jack said, rolling on the floor and pushing himself up in to a squat. A bubble dropped down and he shot right up next to it with his arms over his head. He didn't even have to jump. He grabbed the floor and pulled up fast as hell.

By the time it was my turn I knew what to do. I waited, dove past the bubble and pulled myself in to the supply room. "Hell yeah," I whispered and stood up straight.

Peen-Iz put his dirty fanger to his mouth to shut me up. He walked over to a control panel in the wall and tinkered with the controls. The next phase of his plan was for him to back up the bubbles to draw the guards in to the room.

Me, Fanger and Jack crouched low and duck walked our way behind a stack of supply containers near the door to the guard room. Hunkered down, we watched as bubbles dropped out of the ceiling, scooped up supply containers and sank through the floor. Over the next few seconds, bubbles dropped out of the ceiling faster and faster, eventually ramming in to each other instead of picking up containers.

Peen-Iz backed away from the controls with his arms in the air and weaved through the bubbles, careful not to touch any of them. "Go when I go," he whispered loudly as he squat down behind a stack of containers on the other side of the door from us.

I raised my left hand and gave Peen-Iz a thumbs up. Me, Fanger and Jack help our positions with knives in hand, listening for the guards. Sure as shit the door swung open after a few minutes.

"Not this shit again," one of the guards said as he strutted through the door. Peen-Iz had been sneaking in the supply room and backing up the bubbles ever so often to condition the guards. That sumbitch did have a knack for strategy.

"Don't touch shit," another guard said as he entered. "These here bubbles are set to snatch up what ever they touch."

The first two guards strolled right past us, not even noticing we was hiding behind the containers, and over to the control panel. Two more stepped right inside the room and took positions facing in to the supply room. The last two fellers stood in the guard room with their backs to the door, guarding the entrance.

Without a peep, Peen-Iz darted out from behind the container and raced for the two guards that were halfway to the control panel. While drawing his knife from his right pocket with his right hand, he dropped his left shoulder and rammed the upper back of the guard nearest to him. The guard stumbled forward from the impact and bumped in to the other guard.

In one smooth motion, Peen-Iz swung his right arm through the air and slashed the overall straps on both the guards. Using the moment, he bent forward, raised his left leg and spun in a circle, landing a roundhouse kick that knocked both them sumbitches sideways. Unable to regain their balance, both guards fell in to bubbles, got sucked inside and sank in to The Hole.

Peen-Iz moved so fast that me, Fanger, Jack and the two guards inside the door damn near froze from the surprise. But that didn't last long. Me and Fanger shot out the door, ready to take out two more of them fellers. Just as the sumbitch to the left was turning around, I rammed my right knee in his gut, grabbed the front left strap of his overalls, and slashed that shit with my blade.

Holding on to the guards overalls with both hands, the little space hillbilly was gasping for air from my blow to his belly, I shifted my eyes to the right. Fanger stood there looking down at the other guard on the floor. I twisted my head over my shoulder and looked in the room. Peen-Iz was bending over one of the guards laid out on the floor and cutting both straps on his overalls. Jack had the other sumbitch in a head lock with on of the critter's straps dangling.

"Git'em in the bubbles!" Peen-Iz hollered.

Peen-Iz and Fanger both grabbed the feet of the guards on the floor, pulled them to the center of the room and watched as bubbles dropped down and picked them suckers up. My guy was gasping so hard I walked him in with one hand and shoved him against a bubble. Jack backed up, planted his feet and twisted his hips to the left, tossing his guard right in to the side of a bubble on the floor.

"Hell yeah!" Peen-Iz hollered, jumping around and waving his fist in the air.

The guards floated around in bubbles, two of them out cold and two of them hollering shit we couldn't hear back down at Peen-Iz. Purty soon the bubbles all got back on track and the guards floated one after the other through the floor. According to Peen-Iz, they wouldn't be able to communicate with anybody from The Hole and it would be a while before anybody even noticed they was gone.

"Let's keep movin'," I said, waving my hand to git Peen-Iz's attention.

"This way!" Peen-Iz landed from a jump, waved his right arm and took off out the door.

I fell in behind Peen-Iz, weaving my way through chairs and desks in the guard room, and put both my hands up near my right shoulder as I neared the door on the other side of the room. Without slowing down, I bounced off the door frame, pushing off with both my hands, and spun around to follow Peen-Iz down a long hallway. I looked back over my shoulder and saw Jack slinking along with Fanger bringing up the rear.

Peen-Iz slid to a stop, yanked open a door on his left, and held it open with his right foot. Waving us in with his left hand he said, "Down the stairs."

I raised my arms high and danced through the door on my tippy toes, damn near crashing it to Peen-Iz from my own momentum. Lowering my arms, I regained my balance and bounded down the stairs in three big hops. Soon as I hit the floor, Fanger and Jack landed right next to me.

"Haul ass," Peen-Iz said, at the top of the stairs. He jumped to the floor in one hop, landed like a cat and took off down the hallway.

I didn't say shit and kept on following Peen-Iz through the tunnel. We cut a right turn and a door with a round window sat at the end of a long hallway.

"That's the space port," Peen-Iz said, as he slowed to a fast walk.

Looking around, I held my position behind Peen-Iz until we reached the door. "How's it look?" I said.

Peen-Iz shrugged and crossed his arms, scanning the ships in the port.

All kinda of ships filled the docking bay. Some round like a ball and others more oval shape like an egg. But they was all that same grayish black color. "Holy shit," I said, rubbing my eyes with my right hand. "That's Bill Cooper and Maybelle Turner sinking down out of that ship."

"That's them a'ight," Fanger said. "Clones prolly."

"Nah, that's the real ones," Peen-Iz said. "That's a shuttle from The Tower."

"What the hell does that mean?" I said, turning to look at Peen-Iz.

"The Tower is another prison. The bigguns mostly keep the originals there." Peen-Iz looked at us like we was supposed to know what he was talking about. Noticing we was lost as shit he continued, "Not ever body can be cloned. They gotta have the right DNA. The ones with the right DNA are the originals. The bigguns keep the originals in The Tower in case they need the DNA for more clones."

"They don't look like prisoners," Jack said. "They actually look purty damn happy."

"They're prolly happy as shit," Peen-Iz said. "They brainwash the originals. Make'em believe their wildest dreams came true. You can't convince them no different neither. In fact, they'll prolly turn your asses in if you try."

"We ain't leavin' without tryin'." I crossed my arms and stared at Peen-Iz. Fanger and Jack moved around beside me and joined in the stare down. If something was going on with Bill and Maybelle we wasn't gonna be satisfied unless we saw it for ourselves.

"Shit," Peen-Iz mumbled. "Let's go." He threw his right arm in the air, started running his mouth about some shit and took off down the tunnel.

THE TOWER_

Peen-Iz lead us through the service tunnels again, ducking in to doorways and hiding around corners, avoiding workers, guards or anybody else who might be poking around down there. As we approached an intersection, Peen-Iz looked back over his shoulder and said in a loud whisper, "Keep back."

I raised my right hand and waved Fanger and Jack over to the side. With my body flat against the wall, I bent my left arm and gave Peen-Iz a thumbs up. Fanger leaned forward to look past me and Jack leaned forward even farther to look past both of us as we watched Peen-Iz work.

After standing dead still for a few seconds, Peen-Iz pointed towards the intersection ahead. A shadow bounced in to view from the right side. Without a word, Peen-Iz rolled up on his tippy toes and side stepped fast a shit like a ninja to the corner. With his head turned to the right, he backed up against the wall and waited for some unexpecting critter to pass by.

I didn't take my eyes off Peen-Iz for shit. That sumbitch was so fast if you blinked you'd miss his attack. Next thang I knew, Peen-Iz's left arm hooked through the air and a loud crack echoed down the tunnel.

"Ho. Lee. Shit," me, Fanger and Jack all mumbled. Impressed again with Peen-Iz in warrior mode.

"All clear," Peen-Z whispered loudly and waved us ahead.

I pushed off the wall with my hips, pumped my arms and legs and cut a sharp right around the corner. Peen-Iz stood bent over, cutting the straps on his victims overalls. Without thinking too much about it, I instinctively grabbed the unconscious critter's right foot and started pulling that sumbitch with me. Leaving bodies around was a sure fire way to git caught. Fanger caught up with me, snatched up the critter's left foot and we pulled him along as we followed Peen-Iz down the tunnel.

Several feet ahead of us, Peen-Iz propped a door

open with his left hip and pointed inside. Me and Fanger scooted past him and pulled the knocked out space hillbilly in to the storage closet. Kicking buckets, boxes and containers to the side, we made room for the critter on the floor. Once he fit all the way, we dropped that sumbitch's legs, raced out the door and caught up with Jack and Peen-Iz waiting at the bottom of a staircase that lead up to the surface.

Light as a feather, Peen-Iz bounded up the steps and hunkered down by the glass door. "This is gonna be tricky as shit," he said looking down at the three of us. "The Tower grounds are covered with guards. Our knives ain't gonna be enough. Anybody got any weapons?"

Me and Fanger tapped our pistols on our hips.

"Them ain't gonna do nothing but git us caught." Peen-Iz turned to look out the door and back down at us.

"I got this thang," Jack said, holding the black box he took from the space ship up to Peen-Iz.

"Why you just tellin' me this now?" Peen-Iz snatched the black box outa Jack's hand.

"You just now asked for shit?" Jack said, shrugging and looking at me and Fanger.

"Hot damn!" Peen-Iz flipped the black box

around in his hand. "This here is spot-porter. We coulda used this shit to git outa The Hole."

"It's a what?" I pushed Jack's right shoulder and clenched my jaw.

"A spot-porter." Peen-Iz pushed a button and a little laser light shot out of the box and on the wall. "You point the dot where you wanna go and it transports you there."

Fanger slapped Jack's left shoulder and raised his eyebrows. "Glad we finally figured that shit out."

"I don't know what this outer space shit does." Jack's mouth dangled open. "Can we use it to git in The Tower?"

"Shit yeah." Peen-Iz launched in to a long ass explanation of how the damn thing worked. Basically, you push one button and a bubble surrounds you. Then you point the little laser pointer dot where you wanna go, push another button and it transports you there. The device can transport a single person or small groups. You just gotta all fit in the bubble.

Peen-Iz handed the spot-porter back to Jack. "Mash this button and the bubble will appear. Point the dot at the back wall of the lobby and hit the other button. Once y'all are inside nobody will even notice y'all are there. Ever sumbitch in that place is lost in their own damn world."

"You're not going' with us?" I said, stepping to the side to let Peen-Iz down the stairs.

"Hell no." Peen-Iz turned around and pulled on his beard. "They will notice me in there. I'll hang back. Y'all hurry the hell up."

Me, Fanger and Jack huddled together by the door. "Y'all ready?" Jack said, holding the spot-porter in both hands.

Me and Fanger nodded and Jack pushed the first button. Sure enough, a bubble swished around us. Jack didn't say shit and just pushed the other button. Ever thang went black for a split second and we was standing in the back of The Tower lobby.

I was a little confused for a second but that was about it. Spot-porting didn't feel like nothing really. It was like closing your eyes for a blink and ever thang around you changed when you open your eyes back up again.

"Y'all good?" I said, twisting my head all around.

Fanger and Jack bobbed their heads and darted their eyes around the lobby.

The Tower looked like some kinda fancy condo resort at the beach. All kinda alien critters wandered around just talking and laughing. Some sat at bars spread around the lobby. Others kicked back and drank at tables in little cafes. And a whole shit load of critters screamed and splashed around in the pool out back behind the building. Not one of them sumbitches noticed the three of standing against the wall.

"I'm gittin' a drank," Fanger said, pointing at the nearest bar with his pokey fanger.

Me and Jack followed Fanger, all of us still rotating our shoulders and swiveling our heads all around. My eyes locked on to a big, tall, greenish-colored hairy sumbitch standing behind the bar. He looked like a mix between Big Foot, the Jolly Green Giant and Paul Bunyan. Outa habit, my right hand slapped my hip as we moved closer the bar.

"Whiskey all around," the feller said in raspy voice.

Me, Fanger and Jack all looked at each other confused as shit, not knowing how that sumbitch knew what we wanted. The big feller reached under the bar and grabbed three bottles of whiskey with one hand. With a wink, he slid all three bottles along the bar, timing it just right as we reached the barstools.

"'Preciate it," Fanger said, reaching for one of the bottles.

I lifted my hand off my pistol, gave the bartender a nod and bellied up to the bar. The three of us sat there, swigging whiskey from the bottle and scoping out the critters coming and going from The Tower. Peen-Iz was right as hell. Didn't nobody pay attention to us or even give a shit we was in the place.

"Looky there." Fanger slapped my shoulder with his left hand and pointed with his pokey fanger.

"That's them," I said, taking a big swig of whiskey. Bill Cooper and Maybelle Turner was walking arm and arm through the front entrance.

"Elevator," Fanger said, screwing the lid on his whiskey bottle.

I slid off the bar stool, put my whiskey bottle in my right front pocket and lead the way across the lobby. Fanger and Jack walked up beside me and we moved in to position behind Bill and Maybelle as they waited for the elevator. When the doors opened, Bill and Maybelle pranced on in. Me, Fanger and Jack slipped right in behind them.

"Hey, Bill. Hey, Maybelle," I said, not sure how they would react.

"Lick?" Maybelle said in a high pitched voice. "Is that really you? And Fanger! Hey y'all!" She opened her arms wide and pulled me and Fanger in for a big ass bear hug.

"Who's the skinny feller?" Bill said, bending to look around the three of us.

"This here's Jack," I said, wiggling around and pushing away from Maybelle.

"What are y'all doing here?" Maybelle took a step back, crossed her arms and squeezed her lips tight. "Y'all can't be chosen ones too, can ya?"

"We ain't chosen for shit. Neither are y'all," I said, taking a quick swig of whiskey. "We're all prisoners on this here planet."

"That's a buncha bullshit, sugar." Maybelle uncrossed her arms and put them on her hips. "Don't you follow all my social media? Me and Bill are the chosen ones."

"Maybelle," Bill said, closing his eyes and shaking his head, "Lick and Fanger aren't social media types like us."

"Now, y'all are gonna have to listen." I held my hands up in from of me. "None of the shit here is real. Y'all are brainwashed and these here alien critters invaded Earth."

"Yeah, and y'all was chosen a'ight," Fanger said with a chuckle. "Chosen to be clones."

"Bull. Shit." Maybelle tucked her chin to her chest and looked up at us. "I got over five-hundred million followers and that number goes up ever damn day. Not one of them said shit about some invasion in the comments."

"I can prove it," Jack said pulling his smartphone outa his pocket. "Check this shit out."

"And who are you again?" Maybelle focused on Jack and shot laser beams at him with her eyes.

"I'm Jack. Just look at this shit." Jack tapped the screen on his phone and held it up for Bill and Maybelle to see. One of the clone videos captured by his drone camera played on the screen.

"That's some kinda fake shit one of my influencer competitors musta posted." Maybelle slapped the camera away from her face. "I'm the number one social media influencer on the whole damn planet. And Bill here is Top Cook, Steel Cook, and Master Cook. All at the same time. Only one to ever win all three in the same season."

"That's right." Bill grinned, showing his bleached white teeth. "Just like I always said I'd be. And I got my own show comin' out next season called Bill Cooper Whooped Your Ass in the Kitchen."

"Brainwashed as shit," Fanger said, holding his whiskey bottle up to the light to see how much was left in it.

Peen-Iz wasn't lying. Them buncha dumb,

stankin', worthless asshole sumbitches knew what they was doing. They tapped in to Bill and Maybelle's wildest dreams. Back on Earth, Bill worked down at the Pump 'N Go gas station and convenience store. His big dream was to own a fancy diner and he was always making up new thangs to sell at the food counter. His liver mush sooshee wasn't half bad but most of the other stuff tasted like shit. He swore one day he would git outa the Pump 'N Go, open a diner and wind up on one of them cooking shows he loved to watch on TV.

Maybelle was an even bigger dreamer. All she wanted was to be a social media influencer. She talked nonstop about how many followers she had and was always wanting people to like the shit she posted. She used to come out to the junkyard and take pictures with all the wrecked luxury cars. She had a knack for it too. She could find the right angle to make it look like weren't shit wrong with the vehicle. One time we got a totaled Bentley and she spent damn near two weeks cleaning it and finding the best angles to make it look like it was in good condition. Then she made Fanger take pictures while she struck all kinda poses all around it. Looking good on social media was purty much all she thought about.

"Look here," I said, "y'all gotta come with us.

Them aliens sumbitches is making y'all believe shit that ain't true."

"Bullshit," Maybelle said. "I done told y'all. I'm the number one social media influencer on the planet. Y'all assholes are just jealous."

"I'm tellin' ya," I said, "Y'all are being held prisoner. There making clones outa y'all and attacking Earth with'em."

"Well, if this is prison I believe I'll stay." Bill put his right arm around Maybelle's shoulders and pulled her in for a hug. "We're killing it here."

The elevator opened and Maybelle shrugged Bill's arm off her shoulder. "I was gonna invite y'all for a drank but I thank y'all better just leave now or I might wind up posting shit y'all sumbitches will regret."

I looked over at Fanger. It was clear he stopped giving a shit about rescuing Bill and Maybelle.

"Let'em stay," Fanger said, finishing off his whiskey. "We ain't got time for this shit."

"I'm with Fanger," Jack said.

Maybelle huffed, turned her back on the three of us and stormed off the elevator. Bill stepped between the doors and turned around. "Come back in an hour or so if y'all want. She'll be calmed down by then." Bill held up his right hand, smiling an unnaturally white smile, and waved as the elevator doors closed.

We watched the numbers go down, sipping whiskey and shaking our heads.

"Weird shit," Jack mumbled.

Me and Fanger didn't say shit and just kept on dranking.The elevator stopped, the doors opened and we worked our way through the lobby, smiling and waving at all kinda critters, doing our best to act like we belonged there.

"I'm making a pit stop," Fanger said, pointing to the left.

The big, hairy green feller waved as we got closer to the bar. "Airplane bottles," he said, "A shit ton." He reached under the bar, pulled out handful of little whiskey bottles and set them on the bar.

"'Preciate it," all three of us said at the same time. We stuffed our pockets full and headed for the exit. Once we got to the front door, we looked across the street and Peen-Iz was waving his arms like a sumbitch from behind the glass door, trying to git our attention.

"Ready fellers?" Jack pointed the laser light across the street, through the glass door and on to the wall. When Peen-Iz noticed the red dot bouncing around, he dropped out of sight.

"Let's do it," I said as me and Fanger squeezed up next to Jack. In a blink we was standing on the stairs again.

"What the hell took you sumbitches so long?" Peen-Iz said from the bottom of the stairs. Four space hillbillies laid on the floor at his feet, knocked out cold.

"You good?" I said, realizing one of them sumbitches was naked as shit. I shot my eyes around the tunnel, doing a double take when I noticed Peen-Iz was wearing the naked feller's shiny overalls.

"Yep, foller me." Peen-Iz waved his right hand and took off down the tunnel.

"Wait!" Jack hollered. "Don't we need to hide them sumbitches?"

Peen-Iz slid to a stop and spun around. "We ain't got time. This tunnel is gettin busy as shit."

Me, Fanger, and Jack hopped down the steps, bounced over the four suckers on the floor, and fell in behind Peen-Iz. Running at a full sprint, we hauled ass down the long tunnels. At each corner, Peen-Iz poked his head around before waving us on.

At one of the wider tunnel intersections, Peen-Iz shuffled his feet to stop, raised his right hand and flattened up against the wall. He peeked left around the corner, whipped his head back around to us and said, "Time to whoop ass fellers."

"How many?" I said, sliding up next to Peen-Iz.

Peen-Iz raised his right hand and flashed four fingers. One for each of us to handle.

I inhaled slow and flexed my fangers to get the blood flowing. Fanger and Jack lined up next to me and Peen-Iz and we all stood there listening. The sound of voices and foot steps grew louder as we waited to make our move.

A group of four space hillbillies walked right through the intersection, talking about some shit and not even noticing us against the wall. I exhaled, slightly disappointed I didn't get a chance to whoop some ass, when one of them sumbitches stopped in his tracks and cocked his head to the right to listen.

Peen-Iz shot off the wall, pulled his right arm back, and dove forward, throwing a right cross and pounding the feller listening in the jaw before he could turn around. That sumbitch hadn't even hit the floor when Peen-Iz planted his feet and followed through with a left-handed upper cut. Timing it just right, his fist cracked the chin of another sumbitch as he was jerking his head around to see what happened. The other two fellers jumped high as shit in the air, startled by the attack.

Fanger charged past me, lifted his knees and hopped clean over the first feller Peen-Iz knocked out. Raising his fists as his feet touched down on the floor, Fanger danced in close and threw a left-right combo, knocking the third feller out cold.

Leaning forward, I sprinted toward the fourth feller. Before I got in ass whooping range, a little red dot bounced around on the chest of the only sumbitch left conscious. Next thang I knew Jack was standing between me an my target, swanging his left fist and landing blows on the critters face. The fourth feller bent his knees and sank to the floor. Jack spun around, grinning from ear to ear and holding the spot-porter up in his right hand. I slid to a stop, annoyed I didn't get to do any ass whooping and at the same time impressed by Jack's move with the spot-porter.

"Move out!" Peen-Iz hollered. He took off down the tunnel, not even bothering to cut the overall straps on the knocked-out sumbitches.

Me, Fanger and Jack fell in and followed Peen-Iz through several more tunnels. Halfway between two intersections, Peen-Iz pulled a panel off the wall. "Space port is that way," he said, pointing down a narrow shaft.

Fanger crawled in first, followed by Jack and

then me. Peen-Iz climbed in, replaced the cover he pulled off the wall and brought up the rear. The shaft was long as shit with a little white dot at the end. After crawling for a while, we reached an open area just big enough for all of use to stand up. We crowed together and looked out of a vent cover and in to the space port.

"What now?" I said, adjusting my feet and shoulders.

"We wait." Peen-Iz stared out through the vent, watching ships as the maneuvered through the space port.

Fanger wiggled around and bent his left arm up in front his chest, holding three little whiskey bottles. Me and Jack each took one and we sipped our dranks, watching Peen-Iz watch the space ships.

SUBVERTED_

We waited for a while, all grouped up together, dranking and watching ships come and go from the space port. For some reason Peen-Iz decided to shut the hell up. From what we knew of him he wasn't one to git tight lipped. Something had changed. From the glances me, Fanger and Jack were exchanging between swigs of whiskey, I could tell they sensed it too.

I chugged down a swoller and decided we had waited in silence long enough. "What's the plan, Penis? What're we waiting for?"

"The right ship," Peen-Iz didn't move. He kept his eyes locked on the space port.

"You gotta tell us sumpin'," Jack said. "How we gonna board one of them ships?"

"We'll use the spot-porter." Peen-Iz turned to Jack and stared for a second, shifted his eyes back to the space port and continued, "We gotta go in with the supplies. We'll spot-port over to one of the big ass supply containers. All four of us will ride up on top of the container. Just be sure not to fall off. They count ever thang that goes on the ship. If one of us gits separated and sucked in to the ship they'll know sumpin' is goin' on. Got it?"

"Um, I guess." Jack looked at me and Fanger and frowned a little.

"That's the ship we want right there." Peen-Iz straightened up and pointed. His fanger followed one of the smaller ships as it flew through the port. "They'll rotate crew and run a systems check. Supplies are loaded last. That's when we'll make our move."

Peen-Iz really was acting different as shit. Before he woulda given us a detailed play by play. Now his lips was locked up tight. But none of us pressed him. We just waited some more, sipping our whiskey and watching the activity on the space port.

"They're loading containers," I said, pointing to the ship Peen-Iz wanted to hijack.

"Spot-porter." Peen-Iz held his hand out to Jack.

Jack dug in his pocket with his right hand, pulled out the spot-porter and tossed it to Peen-Iz.

Without another damn word, Peen-Iz pointed the laser dot at a big ass container as we all bunched up together. In a blink we was standing on top of the container. Peen-Iz laid out flat and whispered loudly, "Git your asses down."

Me, Fanger and Jack dropped on our bellies and pressed our arms, legs and heads tight against the container. The damn thang vibrated fast as shit and lifted off the ground. Just like before, we passed through the Jell-O and emerged in the supply room.

Once the vibrating stopped, all four of us slid down the side of the container to the floor. Peen-Iz hustled to the back of the room, raised his right arm and tapped the wall with his fanger. A touch screen appeared and he tapped away doing some shit. It was clear he knew his way around the ship.

After a couple minutes, Peen-Iz turned around and walked back over to us. "This here is a patrol ship. It's small. Fast. Loaded with weapons. And runs with a twenty-man crew."

"What kinda weapons?" I asked.

"Ever thang we need to fight off an attack. But not enough to mount an attack of our own." Peen-Iz crossed his arms and plopped down on a container.

"Our best bet is to go room by room and take the crew out a few a time. Neutralizing the the light suits is critical. If any one of them sumbitches sets off an alarm that's the end. Y'all got it?"

"Hey Penis," Jack said, raising his hand like he was in school. "Can we do that shit to them that they do to us where they lock our bodies up and float us through the air?"

"No," Peen-Iz snapped without saying any more. He bounced off the container and walked to the touch screen on the wall.

"Just to clarify," I said, following Peen-Iz for a couple steps, "we're just whoopin' asses and cuttin' overall straps. That's all we gotta do?"

"Yep," Peen-Iz said with his back turned. "Y'all do that and I'll take care of ever thang else."

I looked back at Fanger. His jaw was clenching up just like mine. Peen-Iz was being light as shit on the details and neither one of us liked it.

"We gotta pass through one empty room," Peen-Iz said, turning around. "The room after that is a guard room manned by four patrolmen. Priority is deactivating the light suits. Let's go." Peen-Iz walked right past the three of us without making eye contact and weaved through the containers to the wall across the room from the touch screen.

I shook my head, looking between Fanger and Jack. We was neck deep in this shit with Peen-Iz. We all knew we didn't have much choice but to keep pushing forward. I spun on my right heel and moved in to position beside Peen-Iz. Fanger and Jack fell in behind me.

Peen-Iz tapped the wall and we all started vibrating fast as shit.

"That's all you gotta do?" Jack said, rubbing his forehead.

"Shut the hell up, Jack," Peen-Iz said, looking straight ahead at the wall.

All together, we stepped in to the wall and passed through the Jell-O in to an empty room.

"Next room's the real deal," Peen-Iz said, running across the room. "Knives on ready."

I slipped my knife outa my right pocket and sprinted over next to Peen-Iz. Fanger and Jack shuffled to a stop next to me and we all held our positions. Peen-Iz gave us a nod, tapped the wall and we vibrated in to the Jell-O.

As my head poked through I knew some shit wasn't right. I lifted my right foot, stepped out of the Jell-O and stood face to face with one of them space hillbilly critters. My reflexes kicked in and my right arm swiped through the air, slashing the left strap of that sumbitches overalls. From the corner of my eye, I saw Fanger, Jack and Peen-Iz bolt away from the wall.

They moved fast as shit but not fast enough. Them other three patrolman slipped their thumbs in their overall straps, pulled forward and activated their light suits. Three light balls shot up in the air and zipped around in front of us.

"Shit! Shit! Shit!" Peen-Iz hollered. "If I wanted to set off the alarm I coulda done that myself!"

"What the hell do we do now?" Jack hollered.

Peen-Iz hooked his thumbs in his overall straps and activated his light suit. His light ball floated up and shot over to the wall on the right side of the room.

I tried to holler but my jaw locked up tight. My arms snapped to my side and my feet lifted off the floor. Not even struggling, I knew from experience I couldn't break free, I locked my eyes on Peen-Iz.

A room like the one Jack found in our ship opened up in the wall. Rows of shelves with little black boxes filled the room. The light ball with Peen-Iz inside streaked through the air and zoomed in to the room. In a flash, one of the shelves was empty and Peen-Iz shot through the wall and out of the room.

Two of the patrolman light balls chased after Peen-Iz. The one left in the room hovered near the ceiling while me, Fanger and Jack floated in the air straight as damn boards. After a few seconds, two more light balls darted in from the left wall and took position next to the sumbitch up at the ceiling.

I was running escape options through my mind when Jack fired off the biggest butt bazooka I ever heard in my life. All three of them light balls vibrated fast as shit and sank down to the floor. Continuing his attack, Jack dropped an ass bomb, followed by a high pitched screamer and then a series of little motor boats.

Me, Jack and Fanger jerked free and hit the floor ready to fight. Fanger bent at his waist and pushed like he was giving birth. He fired off a howler, and chuckled as he worked up another fart. I tensed up my belly, shifted my hips side to side and ripped off a little screecher. Them sumbitches didn't stand a damn chance. Their lights burned out completely and three space hillbillies rolled around on the floor, coughing and gaging.

"Git their light suits!" I hollered.

Fanger pounced on top of one them critters, dug his knee in his chest to keep him from rolling side to side, and unhooked that sumbitches overall straps with his left hand. That critter was choking so bad all Fanger had to do was grab the legs of the light suit and pull.

Jack ripped one more ass blaster and the two of us follered Fanger's lead. We each pinned a critter down, unhooked the straps, and yanked their the light suits off fast as shit. The hardest part was not getting an eye full of man junk.

I shook out my overalls with both hands and looked inside to make sure that space hillbilly didn't leave no skid marks or some shit like that. Satisfied it was mostly clean, I stepped my right foot in then my left and pulled the overalls up to my waist. Running the straps between my thumbs and pointy fangers, I bent my arms back and pulled the straps over my shoulders. The suit was a little tight but I could manage. Soon as I got the straps hooked, I looked over at Fanger and Jack.

Fanger's suit was a wee bit small but fit him good enough. Jack was a different story. These space hill-billy critters were short and stubby sumbitches. Me and Fanger grinned as we watched Jack struggling with his light suit. Wiggling from side to side, he pulled the damn thang up and his legs poked out from the knees down. Then he had to bend over and pull the crotch way up into his junk to git the straps over his shoulders. Once he got the straps hooked he couldn't straighten up all the way without causing some serious damage to his man business. Me and Fanger laughed our asses off at Jack standing there hunched over like an old man.

"I'm testing this shit out." Fanger hooked his thumbs in the straps, pulled forward and a light ball surrounded him. The light bobbed up and down for a second, lifted off the ground and took off. "Yee haw!" Fanger hollered

Not wasting any time, I pulled my straps with my thumbs and a light ball flashed around me. I rocked front to back on my heels and toes and lifted my elbows to shoulder height, feeling the suit out.

"Just lean in to it!" Fanger hollered from over my head. "Use your arms to steer and shit!"

I leaned forward and my feet slid across the floor. Moving around was easy as shit. I shot my arms up over my head and took off like Superman. Surprised at my speed, I lowered my arms back to my side. I stopped moving completely and hovered on the air.

Fanger circled me, twisting in a corkscrew, and laughing his ass off. As I watched, I noticed it didn't even look like he was wearing a light suit. It looked to me like he was flying around on his own.

I laid forward, thrusted my arms up in front of

me and took off. Right before I hit the wall I rolled to the left and turned. I couldn't believe how easy to was to maneuver. It was almost like all I had to do was thank it and it happened.

I flew up next to Fanger and we both looked down at Jack. He was having an all together different experience. Ever time he raised his arms his suit rode up in to his business. He skimmed across the floor, rising and fallen, starting and stopping, and moaning and groaning. He looked up at me and Fanger, his mouth hanging open like he was about to puke.

Me and Fanger pointed down and laughed. I rotated my body, getting set up to ram Jack for fun and two more light balls shot through the ceiling. Outa nowhere the perfect plan popped in to my head. "Blue forty-two!" I hollered to Fanger.

Fanger didn't say shit. He flew in a circle around the edges of the room, picking up speed with each revolution. He knew exactly what to do.

Blue Forty-Two was code for a plan me and Fanger worked up back in the junkyard. We never did figure out how or when we might need to use Blue Forty-Two in a real scenario. Mostly because it was dangerous as shit and had a high likelihood of maiming or killing Fanger. But in the space ship, wearing light suit overalls and under attack by flying space hillbillies, it made sense.

"When I give the signal, you go for the one on the right," I whispered loudly to Jack. "I'll take the one on the left."

Fanger built up so much speed he looked like a blur. Back home we practiced Blue Forty-Two with cars, trucks, RVs, motorcycles, and purty much any thang else that moved. But nothing matched the speed Fanger hit in his light suit. We used to set the vehicles to blow up in the junkyard too. But we was going to have to manage with out any explosions on the space ship.

The plan was doing exactly what it was supposed to do. Confuse the shit outa ever body. Jack looked lost as hell, and them patrolmen sumbitches hovered in the center of the room, looking down at me and Jack and back up at Fanger.

"Brake!" I hollered up at Fanger.

Fanger turned off the light suit, dropped from the ceiling and rolled head over heels across the floor. Both them space hillbilly sumbitches scratched their heads, wondering what the hell was happening.

I took off and zipped in behind the sumbitch on the left, flying up behind him and wrapping my legs around his waist. I bent forward, reached my arms around his chest and slit the straps on his overalls. That sumbitch dropped straight to the floor.

Jack flew up under his target, knife drawn and squealing a little form the pain. Still he caught the critter off guard, slashed his left overall strap and sent that asshole to the floor.

Fanger rolled to his feet, hopped and flew next to me and Jack. The three of us bobbed in the air and looked down at the two sumbitches we just dropped. Next thang we knew, two more light balls flew in from the left and another two from the right.

I adjusted my knife in my right hand, prepping to whoop ass, when the walls started swirling. I rocked side to side and lowered my feet to the floor, stumbling a little from the dizziness. As the walls swirled faster, ever one of them space hilly fellers slapped their arms down by their sides and jerked up straight as damn arrows.

Me, Fanger and Jack all pressed our hands to our ears and dropped to our knees, swimmy headed as hell. The walls, the ceiling and the floor transformed all around us. Little clear balls shot through the air and collected around the stiff ass patrolmen. More and more surrounded them critters until they was all completely covered. A whizzing and whirring sound pierced my ears and I tucked my head in to my chest.

Just when I thought my head would explode the noise stopped.

I lifted my head real slow and shifted my eyes to the left and right. Jack and Fanger were lowering their hands from their ears and looking around too. The ship had transformed in to one big ass open room. All twenty of the crewman were frozen inside a solid clear bubble that floated in the air over the center of the room. Directly under the giant clear ball, Peen-Iz moved around inside a circular control panel, tapping on controls like crazy.

I stood up, lowering my arms and scoping out the room. It was big as shit. Fanger nudged my right arm with his left hand and slapped a little bottle of whiskey in my palm. The three of us stood there, sipping whiskey and watching Peen-Iz ignore us.

"What the hell, Penis?" I said. "You do this shit?"

"Yep, I control this here ship now." Peen-Iz put his hands down flat on the control panel, looked up at us and grinned. "It didn't go exactly like I planned but we got shit done."

"What the hell happened to the crew?" Jack said, staring at Peen-Iz with his head cocked to the side.

"The ship has an anti-mutiny system. Believe it or not, we stole that technology from somewhere. It's designed to restrain the crew and send the ship back to Bom'Kyn. I was able to activate the device and override the navigation to take control of the ship myself."

Peen-Iz seemed to be back to his old talky self. "Looks like you coulda done this shit yourself," I said. "Why the hell did you need us?"

"From experience I know I can handle about ten of these sumbitches in light suits on my own." Peen-Iz titled his head back down towards the controls. "I needed you fellers to distract enough of them so I could git control of the ship."

Me, Fanger and Jack looked at each other, not really sure what the hell to do. "So what's the plan now?"

Peen-Iz pushed off the control panel and backed away, keeping his eyes on the three of us. Walking backwards, he stepped through a little opening in the circular control panel, side stepped to the left and walked around to the front.

"I appreciate the help, fellers." Peen-Iz dug in his pockets with both hands and pulled out two little black boxes, one in each hand. "But I don't really know how much I can trust y'all."

"This ain't good," I said, slapping my right hip.

Peen-Iz bent his right arm and twitched his wrist. A blue laser beam fired out of the black box and swiped past the three of us, cutting the the straps on our overalls. His left thumb pressed a button on the other black box and a big ass Jell-O ball swooshed around us, knocking all three of us on our butts.

On our hands and knees, we all looked through the bottom of the Jell-O ball as we rose up to the ceiling. Below us Peen-Iz went back to work at the control panel.

"Looks like somebody needs an ass whoopin'," Fanger said, twisting open a bottle of whiskey.

Jack squeezed his gut like he was working up a fart. I waved my right hand in the air and said, "Not yet. Let's see what that sumbitch is up to before we make our move."

Me, Fanger and Jack sipped whiskey and watched Peen-Iz doing what ever the hell he was doing down below.

THE ENCOUNTER

BOOK 5

AGREEMENT_

THAT SUMBITCH Peen-Iz went and did it. That asshole double crossed us and trapped me, Fanger and Jack in one of them Jell-O balls. We was all pissed off as hell but we knew whining, complaining and second guessing wouldn't fix shit. We did what we had to do at the time to get out of The Hole and off the planet. The only thing we could do was move forward. Besides, me and Fanger had dealt with our fair share of two-timing assholes back at the junk-yard. We knew how to hold a grudge with patience. And not only did we have the patience for revenge, me and Fanger was trained as shit too. We decided the best strategy was to get back to the basics and work through the problem. Just like we always practiced back on Earth. So "back to basics" was our new motto.

Jack was handling the backstabbing purty good too, even though he didn't have me and Fanger's training. In fact, he didn't even seem to give a shit we was imprisoned. All Jack wanted to do was press his face up against the bottom of the Jell-O ball and look down at Peen-Iz working the controls. While me and Fanger got back to basics, Jack watched ever damn tap and swipe Peen-Iz made on the control panel and learned all kinda shit about how the ship worked.

Peen-Iz either didn't know or didn't care that he was giving Jack a free lesson. That sumbitch ignored the shit out of us and the patrol ship's crew froze up in the solid clear bubble that hovered next to us. But we didn't care he was ignoring us. It gave me and Fanger time to work up our plan and Jack time to learn how to operate the ship.

Like I said, back to basics was the first step. Even though we didn't train in space or on a space ship me and Fanger knew how to operate in unknown environments. When in doubt we always deployed our secret weapon: Get Fanger drunk and wait on the strategizing. I even gave him a couple of my whiskey bottles just to boost his buzz a little. Sure enough that shit worked.

"I know what to do," Fanger said, slipping an empty bottle in his right pocket. "Same shit we do to all them hillbilly alien sumbitches."

Jack lifted his head and looked to the right at Fanger. "What's that?"

"Fart on them sumbitches and whoop their asses." Fanger handed me back one of my full bottles of whiskey. His buzz was strong and he didn't like to hog booze. "Penis ain't never seen us do it neither. He don't know what farts do to assholes like him."

"You're damn right." I twisted the lid off the bottle. "We can vibrate outa here and take that sumbitch by surprise. Jack, you good to fly this here ship?"

"Prolly," Jack said. "I know how to do all kinda shit now."

"Then that's our plan. Alpher Bater Whoop Penis's Ass." I shifted my eyes between Fanger and Jack. "Back to basics works good a shit."

"One thang," Jack said, looking down through the bottom of the Jell-O ball. "Ain't we high as shit? We're gonna hit the floor hard as hell."

Me and Fanger looked at each other, grinned big as shit and both said, "Back to basics."

Back in the junkyard me and Fanger trained doing that par coors thang where you jump off high shit, do flips and roll around. We both were good as hell at jumping from high up and landing without getting hurt. Jack handled himself purty good so me and Fanger sometimes forgot he wasn't trained like us. We gave him a quick down and dirty lesson on how to hit the ground and roll. After a couple practice falls—me and Fanger tossed him in the air and moved outa the way—he hit the curved bottom of the Jell-O ball just fine.

Even though Jack was still nervous as shit about the big drop to the space ship floor, we couldn't practice no more. We were all itching to initiate Alpher Bater Whoop Peen-Iz's Ass, and me and Fanger, and Jack to some degree, were all willing to sacrifice Jack's condition to take out Peen-Iz.

"One more thang." Jack scratched his head with his right middle fanger. "What happens if Penis paralyzes our asses?"

"Fart," Fanger said with a sniff.

"A'ight then. Let's run through it one more time," I said, looking down at Peen-Iz. That sumbitch hadn't looked up at us once to see what was going on. "Fanger goes head to head with Penis. I work my way around behind that sumbitch for back up and Jack you fart your ass off. Especially if we get paralyzed. But remember to stop if we start vibrating through the ship floor."

Fanger and Jack both gave me a thumbs up and moved in to position. Fanger stood dead center in the bottom of the Jell-O ball. I took position on his right and Jack took position on his left. Fanger inhaled a deep breath of the fresh ass air, raised his right arm, clenched his fist and said, "Start rippin'."

Jack fired off an ass bomb and we all chuckled. After a second, we vibrated fast as shit and sank down in to the Jell-O.

Soon as my feet and waist dangled out of the bottom my lower body locked up. Jack called that shit right on the money. It didn't take Peen-Iz long to paralyze us. The upper half of my body vibrated, sank through and locked up stiff as shit as soon as I was out of the Jell-O.

All three of us floated down, arms and legs tight against our bodies while Peen-Iz hollered, "What the hell did y'all dumb shits do?"

We floated down a few more feet and Jack ripped of an ass blaster, breaking our arms and legs free. Jack—probably worried he hadn't quite mastered the par coors shit— timed his fart just right. All three of us dropped the last few feet and rolled on the floor for a soft landing.

"Holy shit!" Peen-Iz hollered, hooking his thumbs in his overall straps. Just as he extended his arms, Jack squeezed out a little poot. Peen-Iz tugged and pulled but his light suit didn't light up for shit.

Fanger pushed himself up with both hands, hopped his feet under his shoulders and shot off like a rocket towards Peen-Iz. Drawing his right arm back, he ran full speed and took a swing at Peen-Iz's head.

Peen-Iz was weak from the farts and distracted a little by his light suit not working right, but that sumbitch still had some fight in him. He ducked down to the left, straightened up, and landed a left hook on Fanger's right jaw.

The blow was enough to throw Fanger off balance but not stop him. Didn't shit stop Fanger when he was pissed off. He jumped in the air, and using the momentum from the punch, spun in a circle like one of them Olympic ice skaters and landed toe to toe with Peen-Iz.

I stepped wide, working my way around to get behind Peen-Iz. Just as I got lined up right behind him Jack fired off a howler. Peen-Iz bent at his knees and damn near toppled to the ground.

Fanger dropped his shoulders and planted his right foot, ready to take off. As his left foot lifted off the ground, Peen-Iz jerked straight as a damn board and floated off the floor. Fanger shot his arms out to the side, shuffle stepped to catch his balance and looked around to see what the hell happened.

"I got him!" Jack hollered, holding a black box in his right hand and pointing it at Peen-Iz.

Fanger spit, straightened up and looked Peen-Iz dead in the eye. "No fun whoopin' your ass when you're weak as shit any how."

"Watch this shit," Jack said, with his right arm stretched out in front and his left hand on his hip. He moved his arm in a Z-formation and Peen-Iz shot to the right, dropped down to the left and shot to the right again.

"Zorro!" Fanger hollered, half way smiling and half way still pissed as hell.

Jack did Zorro a couple more times, spun Peen-Iz around in circles, and flung him around like he was on the end of a whip. Me and Fanger took turns holding the black box and slang Peen-Iz around the the ship too. We laughed our asses off but finally got bored with the show.

"Can you put his ass in the Jell-O ball?" I said.

Jack jogged over the the control panel. I swung my arm in a couple Zorro swishes as I watched Jack tinkering with the controls. He tapped on the panel and the Jell-O ball we was in disappeared.

Jack snatched another black box off the control panel, and with a flick of the wrist he cut the straps on Peen-Iz's light suit with the same blue laser Peen-Iz used on us. In a flash a Jell-O ball appeared around Peen-Iz.

I pushed the button on the side of the black box with my right thumb and Peen-Iz dropped down inside the Jell-O ball. Soon as he got his balance he plopped down on his butt, crossed his arms and legs and looked up at the top of his new prison cell.

"You got any thang to say!" I hollered.

Peen-Iz didn't say shit. He just stared straight up in the air grunting, straining, huffing and puffing. If I didn't know better I'd have swore he was fixing to have himself a baby.

"What the hell is that asshole doing?" Jack said.

"That sumbitch is trying to fart!" Fanger aimed his pokey fanger at Peen-Iz and laughed. "Guess you space hillbilly sumbitches don't got it in ya!"

Me, Fanger and Jack pointed and laughed our asses off at Peen-Iz. He finally gave up, rocked side to side to adjust his position and sat still with his jaw tight and his lips all bunched together.

"What's the status, Jack?" I said, still giggling a

little at Peen-Iz trying to fart.

"Looks like we're in orbit around some planet." Jack stared down at the control panel, watching shit light up all over the place. After a couple seconds of rapid blinking, a TV screen appeared in the wall. "I don't thank I did that shit." Jack held his hands in the air with his fangers spread apart.

A planet zoomed in to view on the TV. The whole damn thang was purple as shit and looked like one of them bouncy balls they sell at the grocery store with a little bit of swirls on the side.

With our eyes locked on the TV, me and Fanger moved around the control panel. I stood with my arms crossed on Jack's left and Fanger leaned his right hip against the work station to Jack's right.

Me and Fanger both turned our attention to the control panel and watched as Jack did shit. Shaking my head, I glanced over at Fanger and he shrugged. Good thang Jack knew what the hell to do. A whirring sound tickled in my ear and I felt the ship move.

"Ship's running a program," Jack mumbled to himself.

The ship passed through the atmosphere and we descended closer towards the surface. Light purple clouds wisped across the TV, opening up a clear view of the planet below. Trees, lakes, rivers, all different shades of purple, grew larger on the screen. From what I could tell, our ship headed for a cluster of dense, purple forest with an open patch in the center covered in long purple grass waving in the breeze. Soon as our vessel sat down on the ground, the walls swirled fast as shit and transformed the ship. One whole wall opened up and a ramp extended down to the grassy surface.

"Ho. Lee. Shit," Jack said. "That looks just like Earth except ever damn thang is purple as shit."

"Where are we?" I said, looking up at Peen-Iz. He didn't say shit. Not a grunt. Not a shake of the head. Nothing. He just stared down at me with his arms crossed and lips still bunched up tight.

"Hey fellers." Jack tapped his pointy fanger on the control panel. "I see a buncha shit headed towards us on the radar."

Me and Fanger stepped around the work station, both of us with our right hands resting on the pistols on our hips, and walked down the ramp side by side. A faint crack popped off in the distance. Then another and another. Little blinks of light flashed like lightening bugs right in front of our faces with a little zinging sound that followed ever damn one of them. The cracks grew louder and changed in to rapid pops with more and more lightning bugs zinging near our heads and torsos.

Fanger turned to me, a shit load of little lights dotting in front of his face, and said, "Bullets?"

"Yep." I squinted at the little light flashes. "Must be a forcefield stoppin'em."

"Look at that shit." Fanger pointed outside with his left hand. The trees and shrubs was swishing around like something was moving through the purple underbrush.

"Git us outa here, Jack." I tapped Fanger on the shoulder with my left hand and we both spun around and walked back up the ramp. "Ain't no sense in fightin' if we don't know what we're fightin' fer."

Jack, head down and back hunched a little, worked the control panel. The ramp swirled and turned back in to the wall of the ship. A whirring sound tickled my ear and I felt the ship jiggle, drift upwards a little and slam down on the ground.

Peen-Iz chuckled. The only sound he'd made since we laughed at his ass for trying to fart. The three of us ignored the two-faced back-stabber.

Jack talked to himself under his breath as he tinkered with the controls. Me and Fanger looked over his shoulder, neither of us able to offer any useful advice. The shipped whirred again and lifted off more steady than before.

"Figured it out," Jack said, wiping little beads of sweat off his forehead with back of his left hand.

I glanced up at the Jell-O ball. Peen-Iz clenched his jaw, rolled up to his feet and paced in circle, shaking his hands like he was about to explode. The ship floated up through the atmosphere and Peen-Iz said, "Don't leave the planet."

"Shut up, dip shit," Fanger said, not turning to look up at Peen-Iz.

"I hid sumpin' on this planet." Peen-Iz had a calm but serious tone in his voice. "I need to git it."

I turned my head up to see Peen-Iz staring down at me, pulling on his long beard with both hands. "We ain't helping you no more," I said. "Sit down and keep quiet."

"Uh, oh," Jack said as the ship whizzed and whirred. "I did sumpin'."

With a jolt, the whirring cut off and the ship rocked from side to side. Me, Fanger and Jack all bent our knees and bounced as the ship swayed and creaked.

"What the hell?" Fanger's eyes darted around the ship.

"That creaking can't be good." I grabbed on to

the side of the control panel to keep my balance.

"Shit, shit, shit." Jacked pounded on the control panel with his pointy fanger.

"Jack got us in to some deep shit," Peen-Iz said from the Jell-O ball. "Y'all are gonna need my help."

I looked to my right at Fanger from to corner of my eye and shook my head.

"Ignore his lying ass." Fanger titled his head down towards the control panel.

I glanced up at Peen-Iz again. He stood with his legs spread and arms crossed, staring down at me between his feet.

"It's a black hole," Peen-Iz said. "Jack flew our asses to the edge of a black hole"

Me and Fanger made eye contact. We trained for a buncha shit but we never trained to escape from a black hole. A tugging feeling grew stronger all over my body, inside and out, and the ship moaned, groaned, and tilted from side to side.

I looked up at Peen-Iz. He stood hunched over a little more than before. "What did you hide on the planet?" I hollered.

Peen-Iz worked his jaw side to side and tugged on his beard with both hands. After a few seconds he straightened his back, stared down at me and said, "It's an invisibility device. I gotta git it."

"He's bullshittin'," Fanger said, looking a little taller and thinner than usual. "He's just fishing for a way to escape."

"Why did ya steal?" Jack hollered, keeping his focus on the control panel.

"Cause it makes shit invisible." Peen-Iz opened his hand, turned up his palms and forced a shrug. "Why the hell else would I steal it?"

"He's just a smart ass." Fanger wobbled a little and and leaned against the control panel.

"I stole it for the bigguns. Then I stole it for myself before I gave it to them." Peen-Iz rubbed his hands and adjusted his stance. "I used to work for the bigguns but I got tired of it. That's all I'll say."

Me, Fanger and Jack twisted our necks to look up at Peen-Iz. That sumbitch knew he was gonna have to tell us more.

"You worked for them buncha dumb, stankin', worthless asshole sumbitches?" I hollered over the noise from the ship.

"Used to until I stole the invisibility device." Peen-Iz looked down with no expression. "That's all y'all need to know."

"You're an asshole." Fanger struggled to raise his last whiskey bottle to his lips with both hands. "We don't trust assholes."

"I'll help y'all but y'all gotta help me," Peen-Iz hollered. His distorted voice drifted past my ears long, deep and drawn out.

The ship juddered, the walls swirled in a murky rainbow pattern, and noises that sounded like a combination of high-pitched screeching and low-pitched humming reverberated all around us. It reminded me of the time me and Fanger got drunk and built a G-force simulator at the junkyard. The queazy sensation in my gut and the complete inability to control my face was purty much the same.

But still this was different than anything me and Fanger ever simulated. The more I looked around the more every thang seemed like it was getting stretched out. Fanger had legs like one of them clowns at the circus that walk on stilts and Jack was so long and skinny he looked like a piece of fishing line with arms trying to control the ship. Even my thanking felt weighted down in my brain.

After several seconds of straining, I was able to turn my eyes up towards Peen-Iz. He was laid out flat on the bottom of the Jell-O ball. The ship rattled and the walls, ceiling and floor swirled and unswirled, alternating between solid black and a hazy rainbow like in an oil spill.

My knees and waist buckled and I dropped to the ground. Fanger splatted down on the floor right next to me. Jack laid out over the top of the control panel, his head turned to the right and squished against the work station surface.

My whole damn face felt like it was sliding of my skull. I made eye contact with Fanger, and we both sat there for a second, pressed flat as shit like two pieces of corrugated cardboard on the floor of the ship.

"A'ight," Fanger grunted.

"We'll help you. Git us outa here!" I hollered.

"Jack!" Peen-Iz said in calm but direct voice, "Do what I say!" Peen-Iz hollered out slightly smothered commands with his face conformed to the bottom of the Jell-O ball.

Jack slid his flat, skinny arms along the top of the panel, executing the commands Peen-Iz hollered down to him.

Just before my innards squeezed through my skin, the ship whirred a muffled whir and the force of gravity ended. Just like that it was all over. I looked at the TV screen and the purple planet blinked in to view.

"We're back," I said, pushing myself off the floor with both hands.

PURPLE_

I BREATHED in a deep breath of the fresh ass air and exhaled. For some reason that close encounter with a black hole reminded me of the junkyard back home. The mild disorientation swimming around in my head had me missing all the training exercises me and Fanger executed over the years. I drew in another deep breath and glanced over at Fanger. From the look on his face I could tell he was feeling nostalgic for the junkyard too. I wasn't used to all that emotional type shit and the feelings creeping up just made me even more determined to run them alien sumbitches off our planet.

Me, Fanger and Jack stood in silence for a while longer, shaking out our hands and feet and looking over our arms and legs as we got used to our bodies being normal again. Without saying a damn thang to each other, the three of us moved out from under the Jell-O ball and huddled next to the TV screen on the wall.

"What do y'all reckon?" I said, keeping my back to Peen-Iz.

"I reckon it's payback time." Fanger pressed on his jaw with his right hand, pokey fanger pointing away from his right eye. "Penis double-crossed us. We double cross him. Simple."

"I know you fellers ain't planning to break our deal," Peen-Iz hollered, almost like he heard what we was saying. "Jack, work the control panel and foller my instructions."

Jack crossed his arms and looked between me and Fanger.

"Just do it, Jack!" Peen-Iz hollered with his arms extended over his head and both hands pressed against the Jell-O ball. "Do what I tell you and you'll learn how to navigate!"

Jack uncrossed his arms, tilted his head to the left and tapped his fangers on his thighs. Peen-Iz hadn't known us long but he sure figured out how to push Jack's buttons. That ole boy was itching to learn how to navigate.

"We're just gonna be stuck in space again if we

don't do sumpin'." Fanger stepped his right foot back, turning to get a look at Peen-Iz.

"Do it, Jack," I said, shaking my head and knowing we might regret it.

Jack twitched and jerked as he hustled over to the control panel with his lanky ass run. Peen-Iz fired off instructions before Jack even got his hands on the work station. Grinning from ear to ear, Jack tapped and swiped away. After a couple minutes a whirring sound tickled my ear and I sensed a little movement. The whirring stopped after a few more seconds and the TV screen blinked on the wall.

"We're just outside y'all's solar system," Peen-Iz said. "We can't git no closer or they'll detect us. From here we look like one of their own patrol ships."

"Ho. Lee. Shit." Jack tapped the controls and pointed to the TV. "That's Earth."

Fanger spun around on his right heel towards the TV. "Hot damn. All them little dots of light ships?"

Jack nodded, tinkered with the controls and the TV zoomed in on Earth. "They got the whole planet surrounded."

We all watched the screen as hundreds of ships zipped around Earth. There was no way in hell we could fight all them sumbitches in our little patrol ship.

I walked over next to Jack and leaned in to his ear. "Is that really, Earth? Or is Penis bullshittin' us?"

"I'm purty sure it's the real deal. I can tell from the position of the planets and shit." Jack tapped the control panel and the image on the TV blinked to a view of the entire solar system.

"All this for our whoop ass device?" I said.

Peen-Iz chuckled a little. "That's why them buncha dumb, stankin', worthless asshole sumbitches put y'all in The Hole. Y'all gotta whoop ass device they wanna steal."

Me, Fanger and Jack glanced at each other and shrugged. It didn't matter no more if Peen-Iz knew about our whoop ass device. We was in too deep a shit for anything to matter.

"Y'all can still run them sumbitches off," Peen-Iz said. "It ain't too late. Long as they got ships on the planet you got time to save your world. Once the ships are gone is when you gotta worry."

"Let's just git this asshole's invisibility device and see what happens." Fanger drew his pistol, checked his bullets and holstered it again. "We can't do shit just sittin' out here in space. We can stab Penis in the back later."

Peen-Iz chuckled again and locked eyes with Fanger. The hate between them two was growing stronger by the minute. But Fanger and me both knew we still needed to milk Peen-Iz for intel. And Jack was happy as shit just to fly the damn space ship.

"Let's go back to the purple planet, Jack," I said, watching Fanger stare down Peen-Iz.

Jack worked the controls with more confidence than before, and he didn't need Peen-Iz to tell him how to get back to the purple planet. That son of a gun learned fast as shit. The whirring sound fluttered past my ear and we was in orbit around the purple planet again in no time flat.

"Where's it at, Penis?" I looked up at the Jell-O ball.

"Pull up the map and run the program, Jack." Peen-Iz broke eye contact with Fanger and watched Jack work the controls.

Jack tapped his fanger and a map flashed up on the wall. A mountain range zoomed in to view on the screen and a red dot flashed at the base of the tallest mountain.

"That ain't where we landed before." I pointed at the map on the wall and looked up at Peen-Iz. "Weren't no mountains around last time."

"The first landing was a decoy landing to draw the purple-necks away from the mountain." Peen-Iz shifted his eyes between me and Jack, ignoring Fanger all together.

"What the hell's a purple-neck?" I said, wrinkling up my forehead.

"Them primitive sumbitches that live on the planet." Peen-Iz shook his head. "They'll whoop y'all's asses good."

"What kinda weapons they got?" I turned my head to the right at Fanger. He was curious too.

"Shit like y'all got on your hips that shoot them little metal balls." Peen-Iz tapped his right hip. "That's what they fired at us the first time we landed."

Me and Fanger cracked half smiles at each other. We both kinda liked the sound of sumpin' familiar for once.

"Y'all should be more worried." Peen-Iz raised his eyebrows. "Purple-necks ain't right in head. They got big ass land vehicles that rumble loud as shit and drive over ever damn thang in their path, they shoot their weapons just for fun and they drink some shit from cans and jars that makes'em lose their damn minds."

"Sounds like my kinda people," Fanger said with a full ass grin on his face.

Peen-Iz ignored Fanger and pointed with his

right pointy fanger up against the Jell-O ball. "The device is in a cave below where that red dot is blinkin'. To get to the cave you gotta move a boulder I put in front of the entrance."

"The device is just sitting there inside the cave?" Jack said, turning his eyes up to Peen-Iz.

"Hell no." Peen-Iz scrunched up his face. "I buried that shit. Y'all gotta dig it up."

"So all we gotta do is find the the mountain, move the boulder and find where to dig up the invisibility device, right?" I drew my pistol, checked my ammo right quick and holstered it again.

"Easy as shit," Fanger said.

"Not exactly. Not with all them purple-necks down there." Peen-Iz pulled on his beard and looked between the three of us. "Y'all need to take me with ya. I can show you how to fight them sumbitches."

"Hell no," I said, waving my left hand in the air. "Me and Fanger will retrieve the invisibility device. Jack will stay back and watch your ass."

"Y'all are gonna want sumpin' to move the boulder," Peen-Iz said. "Open the weapons room, Jack."

Peen-Iz eased off the pressure to take him with us and he was getting to be a little too helpful all the sudden. I was sure that sumbitch was working up some kind of plan. Fanger looked over at me and I could see in his eyes he was thanking the same damn thang. But we just had to go with it for the time being.

Jack worked the controls and the walls swirled. One of them rooms with all the little black boxes on the shelf appeared, and Peen-Iz told us which device to take. I snatched it off the shelf and backed out of the weapons room.

"Watch this fellers." Jack tinkered with the controls and the walls swirled again. The room with the shelves disappeared and a locker room appeared.

"Hot damn." I slapped Jack's right shoulder. There musta been thirty lockers with a light suit hanging in ever damn one of them.

Me and Fanger moseyed over to the locker room and scanned the lockers with all different size suits hung inside. We both walked along, pulling the suits out and checking the sizes. We found our sizes, stepped in to the legs and buttoned the straps over our shoulders.

"Here you go, Jack," Fanger said, tossing a long ass skinny pair of overalls over the top of the control panel. "This outa stay outa your junk."

Jack backed away from the control panel long enough to put on the light suit. Soon as he hooked the straps over his shoulder he hunched over the work station again, lost in his own world. With a swipe of his pointy fanger, the ship whirred and we descended through the atmosphere to where the red dot blinked at the base of the mountain.

"Activate light suits." I hooked my thumbs in the straps and pulled. Fanger and Jack did the same thing. "Comm check."

"I hear ya," Fanger said, lifting off the floor.

"Me too," Jack said, tapping away.

Our voices came through loud and clear with the light suits activated. Jack did sumpin' and the wall swirled, opening the side of the ship to the mountain. No ramp extended this time around, just a big opening to the purple planet.

Me and Fanger was ready as shit to fly in these suits again. We both shot our arms over our heads, leaned forward and flew outside. Fanger leaned and peeled off to the left and I soared off to the right.

I glided low along the surface of the planet, the rocky purple terrain blurring past me as I picked up speed. With a slight tilt of my head upwards, I angled up and climbed higher in the air. Flying in them light suits was easy as shit. I caught a glimpse of Fanger way above me, twisting, flipping, circling and soaring through the purple sky.

"Penis says y'all need to stop messing around and git to the cave," Jack's voice said in my ear.

"Tell him to kiss my ass," Fanger's voice said back. Me and Fanger tested out the light suits for few more minutes just to piss Peen-Iz off, and regrouped over the top of the ship.

"Reckon that's the rock." Fanger pointed to the base of the mountain with his pokey fanger. A big ass boulder with a different shade of purple and texture from the rest of rocks around rested against the base of the mountain.

"How we looking, Jack?" I said, swiveling in a circle and looking out over the forest that stretched out behind us.

"I don't see shit on the scanners," Jack said. "Y'all are clear."

Side by side, me and Fanger flew down to the base of the mountain. Still hovering in the air, Fanger pointed the black box at the boulder, pressed the only button on the device with his thumb, raised his left arm and lifted the damn thang off the ground.

"This thang would be handy in the junkyard." Fanger flicked his wrist and tossed the boulder to the side.

We both rotated around, scoping out the surroundings before darting for the cave entrance. I gave Fanger a nod and we glided right on in to the cave.

"How's it looking fellers?" Jack said.

"Looks like a purple cave to me." Fanger hovered, looking the cave up and down.

Our light suits gave off enough light to see a good distance in front of us. We inched in slow as shit, making sure not to stir any thang up. Peen-Iz could have easily been setting us up for some shit.

"Where to, Jack?" I said.

"Penis says go all the way to the back wall of the cave." Jack's voice come through clear as shit. "It's buried up against the wall. Right in the middle."

Me and Fanger flew in low and slow, walls narrowing the deeper we penetrated the tunnel. But it didn't feel cramped up or stagnant like the caves I'd been in back home. Inside the light suit the air was fresh as shit. Purty soon the walls was so close me and Fanger had to fly single file. Fanger took lead and I brought up the rear.

"Back wall." Fanger pointed with his pokey fanger at the end of the tunnel.

Fanger raised his knees and flew backwards as I dropped down to almost ground level and flew under him. We both knew from experience and training I was the better digger so it just made sense for me to take the lead on the hole digging.

I sank all the way down to the purple cave floor, sat on my knees, and bent forward to get to work. Digging in the light suit was weird as shit. My knees never actually touched the ground and my hands never actually touched the dirt. The light suit created some kinda super thin layer between me and the shit I was touching. If I didn't know better I'd have swore I was covered in a giant rubber glove or some shit. I adapted to the sensation fast enough and scooped up handfuls of the soft, cool purple soil.

"Got sumpin'." I grabbed on to what felt like a box with both hands. I pulled the damn thang up and the purple dirt fell away. Sure as shit I was holding a black box about the size of a shoe box.

"Open that shit up." Fanger twisted back and forth, looking between me and the entrance to the cave.

I lifted the lid off and didn't see shit inside. After scratching my head for a second, I reached my hand in and felt something solid. "The device is invisible," I said over my shoulder.

"Makes sense." Fanger moved slow towards the entrance.

Tapping and squeezing, I determined the gadget

was disc shaped and about the size of an average cow patty. Holding on to the device with my right hand, I pulled the big front pocket on the bib of my overalls open with my left pointy fanger and bent my right elbow.

"What the hell?" I rubbed the device against my chest, unable to get the disc through the light suit barrier. "It won't go in my pocket."

I kept pressing the device against my chest but the the damn thang never slipped in to the pocket. After a minute of struggling Jack's voice came through the comms, "Penis says you gotta turn the light suit off, put the device in the pocket then turn that shit back on again."

Peen-Iz advising me to turn my light suit off on an alien planet didn't exactly feel right. But if he was planning some shit I figured it was best to go ahead and get it over with. So really I didn't have a choice but to follow his instructions despite my better instincts.

Fanger glanced back over his shoulder, probably sensing what I was thinking, and gave me a nod. "It's all clear," he said, turning back towards the cave entrance. "Do that shit."

I hooked my thumbs in the straps, the device still in my right hand, and pulled forward. My light suit blinked off and the dank ass cave air surrounded me. I took in a slow breath, unsure how the air would feel in lungs. After a pause I exhaled. The air wasn't nearly as fresh and clean as the air on the ship but it didn't hurt none neither. I shoved the device in my chest pocket and pulled the straps, reactivating my light suit. I figured Peen-Iz musta planned this round to try and build our trust.

"Device recovered," I said, floating up and straightening my legs. "Heading back to the ship."

"Ten four," Fanger and Jack said at the same time.

Me and Fanger flew back to the entrance. Just as the tunnel widened enough for us to fly side by side a muffled clank rang through my light suit. I looked at Fanger and little lightning bugs blinked all around him. The clanking stopped for a second then grew fast as shit.

"I thank we're under fire," Fanger said. "These here light suits are absorbing shit."

Me and Fanger kept moving forward until lightning bugs and muffled clanking was all we could see and hear. I squinted real tight and saw three purple sumbitches on the ground pointing what looked like riffles at us and popping off rounds.

"Jack!" I hollered. "You see this shit?"

"See what shit?" Jack said.

"Three purple sumbitches are shooting at us!" I hollered.

"I don't see shit on the scanners." Jack sounded confused.

Fanger drew his pistol and fired off a round, hitting one of them purple critters right in the chest. The sumbitch fell back on the ground, stopped moving for a second then took in a deep breath. The damn critter rolled over, grabbed his riffle, stood back up on his feet and opened fire again.

"Keep shootin'!" I drew my pistol and me and Fanger squeezed off a few rounds, taking out all three of them assholes. But them sumbitches didn't stay down. They all took a deep breath, got back on their feet and opened fire.

"Purple-necks!" Fanger hollered, holstering his pistol.

"Penis says them are scouts," Jack said. "He says git your asses back to the ship. There's a shit ton on the scanners now headed your way. They'll be on your asses in about five minutes."

I raised my right arm, clenched my fist and hollered, "Make a break for the ship!"

Me and Fanger leaned forward and zipped right past them purple-neck sumbitches with bullets peppering our light bubbles. Soon as we shot through the entrance, Fanger whipped around and aimed the black box with his left hand at the big ass boulder that was blocking the entrance. Twisting his wrist, he picked up the boulder and dropped it in front of the cave, trapping them sumbitches inside.

"Y'all git your asses in here!" Jack hollered.

Me and Fanger stretched our arms out like Superman and took off like lightning bolts. A rocket hissed through the air and exploded between us and the ship, blasting me and Fanger back towards the mountain.

My light suit absorbed most of the impact, but the force of the blast jarred me around enough to disorient me for a couple seconds. "You good, Fanger?" I said, trying to catch my balance in the air.

"Yep, more incoming!" Fanger hollered.

Extending my arms to the side, I stabilized myself just in time to see another rocket heading straight towards me. Outa no where, Fanger rammed me from the right side and pushed me out of the line of fire. The rocket exploded and the two of us flipped through the air, neither one of us in control.

"Lick!" Fanger hollered.

I couldn't see shit. All I knew was we were drifting like dust balls in the wind. I blinked and caught a glimpse of a giant ass net dropping down from above. After a swish, me and Fanger slammed together face to face, our light suit bubbles separating us by inches.

"Sumpin' caught our asses," Fanger said, pushing away from me with his hands and feet, making space between us.

I pushed back, creating enough room for us to move around like two goldfish in a tiny ass bowl. But that didn't last long. The net tightened and closed in on us, mashing us tight together until we was purty much pressed right up against each other.

My right hand went for my hip but I stopped myself. Weren't no sense in wasting ammo. I bent my arms and patted my chest. The invisibility device was still there safe and secure. "Jack, what's your status?" I hollered.

"Hell if I know!" Jack hollered back. "The ship won't move for shit!"

"Look at that shit," Fanger said, looking up above us.

A giant net draped over the top of the patrol ship.

"What the hell are we caught in?" Jack hollered.

"Big ass nets!" I adjusted to keep from getting too

close to Fanger. "Were caught in a trap. Penis know anything about this?"

"I don't think so. He's pissed as hell hollering all kinda shit at me." Jack's voice faded.

"Jack? You there?" I looked at Fanger "Jack! What the hell?"

Jack didn't respond.

Fanger lowered his head, looked at me and said, "They jammed our comms."

"Purple-necks," I mumbled under my breath.

THE SIMILARITIES_

Me and Fanger kinda levitated inside the net. Our light suits musta initiated some sorta safety protocol cause they was keeping us and the net floating in the air without us doing shit. I wiggled and Fanger squirmed to position ourselves side by side. Trapped like a couple bugs, we sat in silence for a few minutes, both of us taking in our situation.

The patrol ship, caught in a big ass net too, bobbed up and down off in the distance. Thick cables, twenty or thirty of them I reckoned, dangled from the bottom of the hefty mesh snare detaining the ship. My eyes followed the cables down and from what I could tell they was anchored to the mountain.

"Looks like an ambush to me." I turned my head

to the right towards Fanger. "No way in hell they had these nets and cables just laying around."

"Sure as hell looks like they was expecting us." Fanger nodded and stared down at the ground below. "We're surrounded as shit now."

I tilted my head down and looked through the bottom of the net. A whole ass ton of purple critters scurried around underneath. The buzzing of power tools, pounding of hammers and the rattling of metal bits and pieces echoed through the mountains. Them sumbitches moved with precision down below, passing tools and tugging in unison on the cables connected to our trap. Them purple suckers worked together like they was trained for this shit. A clear sign we was ambushed.

A low, deep rumble roared out of no damn where. Me and Fanger wrenched our necks from side to side, hunting for where the noise was coming from. Next thang I knew a big ass vehicle, kind of mix between a tank and a monster truck, bounced up out of the woods and on the clearing at the base of the mountain. The thundering beast of a ride circled the group of purple-necks—at least I assumed them critters was purple-necks since they was all purple as shit— revving the engine and whipping the ass end around. Ever one of them sumbitches hooted and hollered ever time the vehicle kicked up purple dust.

The monster truck tank thang skidded to a stop in the middle of the clearing, and the purple-necks on the ground grouped up in to little clusters around the six cables that ran from the base of the mountain to the net me and Fanger was trapped in. Working in teams, them sumbitches grunted and groaned as they lifted the cables out of brackets connecting them to the mountain. The net swayed from side to side as them purple fellers lugged the cables over to the vehicle and clipped them in to huge brackets that ran along the side of the truck tank. They was damn sure trained as shit for that maneuver.

Me and Fanger looked at each other with our jaws dangling wide open. The engine revved, the vehicle took off and the slack in the cables tightened up, jerking me and Fanger a little. Our light suits absorbed most of the impact and we didn't get nearly the whiplash I woulda expected from the force of the tugging.

The monster truck tank screamed like a banshee until it reached the end of the clearing. Then after a little bit of a pause, the front end nose dived, the ass end shot straight up in the air and the vehicle hauled ass down the step hill leading in to the purple forest below. That rascal pulled me and Fanger along like we was parasailing behind one of them big ass boats we used to see at the lake.

The engine growled and roared and the truck tank rocked and rolled over ever thang in its path, pulling us so fast the cables stretched out and we dropped down level with the back of the vehicle. Purple tree limbs slapped against the side of the net and clouds of purple dust drifted around the outsides of our light suit bubbles.

"If we wasn't captured this would be fun as shit," Fanger said with a smile.

Not knowing what else to do me and Fanger bother hollered, "Yee haw!"

After several minutes of our net getting pummeled by tree limbs, shrubs and other debris kicked up by the monster truck tank, the vehicle gasped and the engine idled down. Me and Fanger shot over the top of the truck tank and snapped back again, our light suits still protecting us from the worst of the whipping back and forth.

The slanging around disoriented me slightly but I spotted the front of our tow vehicle angling up to climb a step hill. The slack in the cable tightened up, yanking us again, and after a buncha bumps and tugs, the truck tank bolted out of the woods and in to another clearing.

I jiggled my butt and twisted my shoulders to look frontwards. Off in the distance sat a cluster of what looked like purple double-wide trailers. The monster truck tank rolled in slow, revving the engine and bouncing the front of the vehicle up and down. The faint sound of hooting and hollering grew louder as we approached the alien trailer park.

"I'm kinda startin' to like this shit." Fanger raised his eyebrows and cracked an even bigger grin.

The monster truck tank skidded to a stop smack in the middle of the trailer park. Me and Fanger got flung over the top of the vehicle again from our own momentum and then snapped back behind it. A spinning noise screeched from below, our net started to sink and I shifted my hips back to look down between my legs. Them sumbitches was reeling us in with a winch.

As we got closer to the ground I got a better look at them purple-necks. Ever damn one of them was wearing work books, jean shorts, and a t-shirt with pictures of different monster truck tanks on them. The net dropped lower, twisting from side to side, and I noticed ever sumbitch in sight had a weapon that resembled a pistol strapped to their hip. Still sinking down, I blinked fast as shit, scanning the crowd, and didn't see nothing but different shades of purple mullets flowing off their heads.

The more they reeled in our cables, the more I damn near rubbed my eyes out with my both my pointy fangers to make sure I was seeing right. Them sumbitches weren't just solid purple. Ever one of them had skin that looked like a different pattern of purple plaid flannel. They even had flaps of what I figured was purple plaid skin poking out of their t-shirts like collars on a flannel shirt.

"Looks kinda like the flannel shirt section of Walmart, don't it?" Fanger said, noticing all my squinting and eye rubbing.

"Musta been a sale on purple," I said with a chuckle.

The squealing from the winch cut off and we hovered over the bed of the monster truck tank. More engines revved off in the distance and the rumbling grew so loud my man junk vibrated just like at monster truck rallies back home. The familiar sensation made me a little homesick for Earth again but that didn't last long. From all sides of the woods, monster truck tanks roared up on to the clearing, bouncing around and kicking up dust. Ever damn one of them whipped the ass end around a couple times then parked in a big circle in the middle of the trailer park.

Purple-necks dropped down from the vehicles and poured out of the trailers, toting what looked like coolers and grills. Sure as shit them sumbitches cracked open cans, lit the grills and set up camping chairs around the monster truck tanks. I couldn't believe my eyes. Them sumbitches was tailgating and shit.

"I'll take one of them!" Fanger hollered down to one of them critters. The purple-necks couldn't see us with our light suits activated but that didn't matter none. A can soared through the air, clanked and disappeared in to the light bubble.

I waved my arms over my head—it seemed like the right thang to do even though I was hidden inside the light—and hollered, "Try again! And I'll take one too!"

Them purple-necks was more than happy to share. Cans flew at us from ever direction, clanking and then vanishing in to the light bubbles surrounding us.

Me and Fanger was thanking the same damn thang. We hooked our thumbs in our overall straps and pulled forward. Our light suits blinked off and cans pelted us in our heads, backs, bellies and rear ends but we didn't give a damn. In just a matter of seconds, we both pulled our straps and reactivated our light bubbles before we sank too far down. In a flash we was hovering again with a shit ton of beer cans floating inside the light bubbles with us.

Me and Fanger didn't hesitate for shit. We both grabbed a can outa the air, cracked it open and kicked our heads back, chugging the liquid down in a few big swollers.

"Taste just like cheap beer." Fanger wiped his mouth with the back of his right hand, pointy fanger out of course.

"Just like home," I said, cracking open another can.

We musta each drank eight or nine each before we even looked at each other.

"This shit ain't half bad," Fanger said between burps.

"I'm gonna make contact." I finished my last swoller and hollered, "Hey purple fellers! Why y'all got us trapped up in here?"

"We figured y'all was a couple assholes!" a voice hollered back.

"Why is that?" I hollered, glancing over at Fanger.

"Cause ever time one of them ships comes here it's full of assholes!" the voice replied.

"That ain't our ship!" I looked down at the purple-necks circling the vehicle. "We stole that shit! We got the crew locked up inside! Let us outa here so we can talk!"

All the hooting and hollering stopped. Them purple-necks huddled around even closer to the monster truck tank and looked up at us. One of them, the leader I reckoned, climbed up on the back of the truck and said, "Turn them lights off and keep'em off some we can see y'all's asses."

I stared down at him for a second. Something about him was familiar as shit but I couldn't put my fanger on it. "Might as well, right?" I said turning to Fanger.

We sipped beers and nodded at each other. Then Fanger hooked his thumbs in the straps, pulled forward and dropped down to the bottom of the net. I pulled my straps with my thumbs and dropped down beside Fanger. Next thang I knew the net opened up and me and Fanger both dropped like turds in to the bed of the truck tank.

Ever one of them purple-necks gasped as we rolled up to our knees. Beers cracked open and voices chattered loud as shit all around us.

"Them ain't Bom'Kynians," I heard one voice say.

"Ho. Lee. Shit," another one said from somewhere. "Look at them. That shit ain't right."

The leader feller dropped off the back of vehicle before I could good a good look at him and hollered from the ground, "Y'all hop down here nice and slow."

Me and Fanger stood up all the way, real slow with our hands out to the side, and looked out over the crowd. The sound of pistols cocking and shotguns pumping filled the awkward silence. Ever damn one of them, even the ones that look like kid purple-necks, pointed a weapon at us.

My eyes shifted around and landed on the feller that jumped up on the back of the truck. Me and him locked eyes, both of us trying to figure out what the hell was so familiar about the other one. From the corner of my right eye I saw another feller walk up to the vehicle. That sumbitch and Fanger was caught in a staring contest too.

The crowd of purple-necks oohed and aahed, letting their weapons sank down slightly. Ever damn critter in the trailer park gawked at me and Fanger eyeballing them two fellers right below us.

I nudged Fanger with my right elbow, neither

one of us breaking eye contact for shit. We both lifted our right foot, took one step forward to edge of the truck tank bed, bent our knees slow as shit and hopped forward, dropping down to the ground. Side by side we stood up straight and puffed out our chests a little as them other two sumbitches stepped up a couple feet away. Not once did any of the four of us blink an eye and break the stare-down.

My mouth dropped open and I couldn't keep my jaw from swanging. Without even looking I knew Fanger's jaw was dangling too.

"Double-gangers," me and Fanger whispered at the same time.

That sumbitch standing right in front of me was my spittin' image if I was made outa purple flannel. And the feller across from of Fanger was his purple plaid alien space twin for damn sure.

The crowd went silent and the more handsome of two fellers said, "My name's Pick. They call me Pick cause when I was a baby I picked my nose all the time."

"Ho. Lee. Shit." I damn near shit my britches. "My name's Lick cause I used lick ever thang." Me and Pick stood there checking each other out from head to toe.

I glanced over at Fanger and he was still in shock.

After a few more seconds of staring, he bent his right arm real slow and raised his right hand in front of his face, wagging his pokey panky in the air.

That other feller bent his right arm too, raised his hand to his face and waved a pokey rang fanger. "Names Rang-er," he said. "When I was kid I broke my rang fanger on my right hand and my mom and deddy didn't git it fixed right."

"Same shit here 'sept they call me Fanger." Fanger extended his right hand and hooked pokey fangers with Rang-er. Them two grinned from ear to ear, tugging fangers back and forth.

"Let's drank," Rang-er said, pulling a jar of clear liquid out of his left pocket. He spun the lid off, took a swoller from the jar, passed it to Fanger and shook his pokey rang fanger in the air.

Fanger bent his left elbow, kicked his head back, and took a big ass swig. "Moonshine I think," Fanger said, passing me the jar.

I wrapped my right fangers around the jar of shine, raised my right arm in the air and turned to crowd. Ever damn one of them hooted, hollered and fired their weapons in celebration. At that moment I stopped missing Earth and the junkyard so much. I lowered the jar, sucked down a big ass swoller and hollered, "Hell yeah!"

"Y'all sure as shit ain't Bom'Kynian," Pick said as I passed him the jar. "Where y'all from?"

"Earth." Fanger twitched his right arm and snatched a can of beer that came flying through air.

"That near Bom'Kyn?" Rang-er cracked a beer, shot his arm out straight and tapped his can against Fanger's.

"Shit if we know." I ducked slightly to the left and snagged a beer headed straight for my head with my right hand. "We don't know shit about where shit is in space. What planet is this?"

"This here's Fla'Nel." Pick said.

"That near Bom'Kyn?" Fanger glanced over at Rang-er and grinned.

"Close enough they fly their ships full of assholes round here purty regular." Pick screwed the lid back on the empty moonshine jar and slapped my right shoulder with his left hand. "Y'all git in the back of the trank."

"Trank," I said to Fanger, swigging my beer. "Makes sense."

"Yep." Fanger nodded, thrusting his right hand out and catching a beer that flew in from somewhere.

Pick and Rang-er hauled ass to the front of the trank parked next to the one that towed us to the trailer park with Pick heading for the driver's side and Rang-er riding shotgun. Me and Fanger hustled to the back of the vehicle, raised our arms over our heads and grabbed on to the open tailgate with both hands. Hopping at the same time, we both pulled up and balanced our hips on the edge of the tailgate. I kicked my left foot up and Fanger kicked his right foot up, hooking our legs on the bed of trank. Crawling our hands forward, we pushed up with our arms and stood up all the way.

"Hot damn." Fanger pointed to a huge cooler right up against the trank cab.

The rear window opened and Pick poked his face through. "Y'all drank all the beer y'all want."

He didn't have to tell me and Fanger twice. I flipped the cooler lid open with my right hand, grabbed a couple cold ones and tossed a can to Fanger. We plopped down next the cooler, me on the driver's side and Fanger on the passenger side, and chugged down our beers.

"Hang on!" Rang-er hollered from the trank cab.

Me and Fanger scooted our backs against the trank bed, both with one arm resting on the cooler, cracked open fresh beers and braced for the ride. The trank roared and damn near shook my drank outa my hand. The engine huffed and puffed, the vehicle danced around underneath us and the front end lifted off the ground. With a thunderous growl, the the trank shot forward, lifting me and Fanger's butts off the bed of the trank. We shot our arms out to the side, dug our heels in and leaned back hard as we could, spilling beer ever damn where.

"Hell yeah!" we hollered as the trank shot off in to the woods. "Yee haw!"

Me and Fanger wiggled our backs and butts back in to seated positions, relaxed our shoulders and enjoyed the ride. As the trank worked its way through the woods, I sipped my beer and took in the view. Ever thang around us looked just like purple versions of nature and shit back home. I even saw a purple flannel squirrel haul ass up a tree.

The combination of beer, moonshine and the bouncing around in the back of the trank relaxed the shit outa me. I took a deep breath and noticed again the air wasn't fresh as shit like on the space ships and on Bom'Kyn. I exhaled, tapping on my beer can with my right pointy fanger. The fresh air was nice but beer and moonshine was better. I reckoned I liked Fla'Nel the best so far outa the planets we'd been to. I drifted back in to my thoughts, just dranking and looking around.

Next thang I knew the trank bounced up in to the clearing where the purple-necks had captured us.

My head jerked to the left as the vehicle whipped around and I spotted the patrol ship still hovering off in the distance inside the giant net. In a cloud of purple dust, the trank skidded to a stop and the engine went silent. The front doors flew open and Pick and Ranger dropped down to the ground.

Me and Fanger stood up, waving purple dust out of our faces. Rotating our heads from side to side, we watched as tranks rolled up and in to the clearing. At the same time, we both titled our heads up to the sky and focused in on the patrol ship.

"What's the plan, Pick?" I hollered, not taking my eyes off the ship.

"We're fixin' to blow up that ship y'all stole!" Pick hollered back.

Me and Fanger sipped our beers, calm and cool on the outside, shifting our eyes between each other, the patrol ship and the crowd forming in the clearing. But on the inside our wheels was turning. We was damn sure gonna have to talk Pick in to letting Jack get off the ship.

Fanger picked up the pace, cracking beers and chugging them down. I knew exactly what he was doing.

"Back to basics," I whispered, watching and waiting for Fanger to work up some strategy.

ALLIES_

Me and Fanger repositioned ourselves on the ground level and leaned against the passenger side door of the trank, pounding beers and watching the purple-necks rolling up to the clearing in all different kinda vehicles. From the sound of all the rumbling way off in the distance, they was coming from miles around. Blowing up the patrol ship musta been topping the list of the day's entertainment.

We loved blowing shit up for fun but this particular explosive spectacle put me and Fanger in one hell of pickle. For one thang Jack was still on the ship. Getting him off safe was our number one priority. Then we had to worry about the ship itself. We didn't have no other way to get back to Earth and run them alien sumbitches off our planet. And mixed in with all the other shit was the fact the we needed Peen-Iz to help us fight them buncha dumb, stankin', worthless asshole sumbitches.

Down below in the purple forest—we could see for miles from the clearing at the base of the mountain—vehicles snaked through the trees towards us from all directions. We figured we had at least until ever body got here to work out a plan. So while the purple-necks was all still arriving, me and Fanger kept on getting back to basics. Both of us pounded one beer after another waiting on the strategy to come to Fanger.

"These here purple-necks seem like decent people," I said between swollers.

"Yep," Fanger burped. He musta a had a good plan forming. He never talked much when he was absorbed in strategizing.

"They like monster trucks, drank beer, cook on the grill, and raise all kinda hell with their weapons when they drank." I kept on talking cause I knew he was listening. "If not for the blowing up the space ship with Jack in it part I'd feel right at home. We even met our double-gangers."

"Yep," Fanger burped again. "I gotta plan."

"Hell yeah." I pushed off the trank with my hips. "What's the plan?"

"We tell them the truth." Fanger ran his tongue on the inside of his right cheek.

"A'ight," I said looking around. "You mean ever thang?"

"Most ever thang." Fanger spit, took a swig of his beer and pointed his pokey fanger at my chest.

"I damn near forgot about this thang." I bent my right arm and patted the front pocket on the bib of my overalls. "Yeah, let's keep the invisibility device to ourselves for now."

"Reckon we outa git to it." Fanger cracked a beer and pushed off the trank with his hips.

I raised my right arm and hollered, "Hey Pick! Rang-er!"

Pick and Rang-er, standing with the crowd milling around under the cables dangling from the patrol ship, spun around to look at me. Pick gave me a nod and the two of them moseyed over, sipping beers and talking to each other about some shit.

"We need to talk to you fellers," I said once they got close. "Our buddy Jack is on the ship."

Pick and Rang-er looked at each other then back to me and Fanger.

"We'll unjam your comms," Pick said. "Tell him to come out real slow."

I hooked my thumbs in my overall straps,

wondering what the hell to do with Peen-Iz and the crew. I took a gander at Fanger and knew right away what he was thanking. All our training had given us a deep mental connection. We was both thanking it was best to listen to our instincts, keep cool and take thangs one step at a time. Once we got Jack off the ship we could tell Pick and Rang-er more.

"I gotta turn my light suit on y'all." I kept my voice real calm and didn't make no sudden movements.

Pick and Rang-er was listening to their instincts too and keeping cool. And since they was just like me and Fanger, I knew they was ready to draw their pistols in a flash. I couldn't blame them neither. If we met them on Earth, me and Fanger would be just as cautious.

"Turn that shit on and talk to your buddy." Pick gave me a nod.

I straightened my arms, pulled the straps with my thumbs and my light bubble surrounded me. "Jack, what's your status."

"Stuck inside this damn net like a fish or some shit." Jack's voice came through loud and clear. "What the hell's goin' on?"

"We gotta git you out. These here purple-necks

wanna blow the ship up" I kept my eye on Pick and Rang-er the whole damn time.

"Say what?" Jack's voice cracked a little. "You gonna let'em?"

"Me and Fanger got drunk and worked up a plan." Jack was nervous but I knew he could handle shit. "Just foller our lead."

"What did y'all drank?" Jack's anxiety turned to curiosity.

"Space beer. We'll git you some. Just don't get distracted."

"A'ight, but what about Penis?" Jack's lip smacking lapped through on the comms. "I can't risk leaving his ass in here alone."

Jack was right about that shit. Not keeping eyes on Peen-Iz was a huge threat. "Freeze his ass and bring him with you."

"And the crew?" Jack said.

"Just bring Penis out for now. We'll worry about the crew later."

"Ten four." Jack sounded a little confused.

I pulled my straps and the light bubble blinked away. "He's coming out and he's bringing one of our prisoners."

Pick and Rang-er gave me thumbs up with their

left hands and slide their right hands over to their right hips, resting them on their weapons.

Me and Fanger stood side by side, our heads tilted up and eyes on the ship. Ever purple-neck in the clearing did the same damn thang. A buncha them fellers who had climbed the side of the mountain to get a view of the ship exploding was pointing and gawking, waiting in expectation.

The side of the ship opened and a ramp extended, ramming in to the net and retracting a couple of times. Pick waved his arms at some feller by the base of the mountain. That feller waved his arms and the cables spread apart, making space for the ramp to extend all the way. The ramp shot out again, hanging off the ship in to thin air. Pick waved his arm again, the feller at the mountain waved his arms again too and a winch screamed, reeling the ship to the surface.

After a shit ton of screeching from the winch and guns firing for no reason, the ramp made contact with the ground. Pick slapped my shoulder, Rang-er slapped Fanger's shoulder and the four of us walked slow and steady to the bottom of the ramp.

Jack poked his head out and ducked back in. I glanced over at Fanger with a grin and then hollered, "Come on out, Jack!"

Jack peeked outside, his eyes darted all around, then he stepped out on to the ramp with his arms in the air, squeezing a little black box tight in his right hand. Purty much just sliding his feet along and taking it one tiny step at a time, he moved down the ramp staring down me and Fanger. At about half way down, Peen-Iz floated in to the opening on the side of the ship, locked up stiff as shit with is arms by his side.

Pick and Rang-er jerked their right arms fast as shit, drawing their pistols off their hips almost as fast and me and Fanger would have. Guns cocked all around and ever thang went silent. Pick leaned his head towards me, fought back a chuckle and said, "Is that Penis?"

"Shit yeah." I snickered a little and held my open right hand up towards Jack. "Penis is our prisoner."

Me, Fanger, Pick and Rang-er busted out laughing. No matter the situation Peen-Iz's name was funny as shit. No surprise our double-gangers thought so too.

Rang-er let out a sigh, tightened his grip on his pistol and got back to business. "Y'all didn't capture his ass. That sumbitch just made you thank you did."

"How the hell do you fellers know Penis?" I said, keeping my eyes on Jack. He stood there looking

back all bug-eyed so I gave him a nod for some reas-
surance.

"Ever body knows Penis." Pick frowned with the
right side of his mouth. "He's Bom'Kynian. That
sumbitch steals ever thang he gits his hands on."

Fanger shook his head and cracked open a beer.
"I got dibs on beating his ass."

"You and me both," Rang-er said, holstering his
weapon a cracking open a beer for himself.

"Y'all want me to come on down or what?" Jack
hollered.

I closed my right fist, lowered my hand down to
my pistol on my right hip, and Jack started sliding his
feet again. I turned to Pick and said, "We met Penis
in The Hole on Bom'Kyn. He helped us escape."

"He was prolly planted there by the Bom'Kyn
leader assholes." Pick raised his eyebrows real big,
contorting the lines that made up the plaid flannel
pattern of his skin, and turned to me. "I bet y'all got
some shit they wanna steal."

"Yep," me and Fanger both said kinda low and
quite.

Pick didn't ask for no details. He just shook his
head and said, "Penis prolly even planned ever thang
that happened to y'all since the first time y'all met.
That sumbitch is devious as shit."

"Don't trust Penis for shit." Rang-er sniffed, spit and tossed me a cold one. "Even other Bom'Kynians don't trust his ass."

Jack reached the bottom of the ramp, his jaw drooping and eyes bouncing fast as shit from me to Pick and Fanger to Rang-er. He pressed his lips close together for a second like he was gonna say something then just let his jaw sag back down.

"Double-gangers." Fanger cracked open a beer and passed it to Jack.

Jack sipped his beer with this left hand, squeezing his eyes open and closed like he was just waking up from a weird ass dream. He let his right arm bend a little and Peen-Iz shot up in to the air over his head like a balloon.

I didn't take the time to explain shit to Jack. I wanted more intel on Peen-Iz. "Y'all thank Penis planned this shit right here? I mean ever thang that's happening right now."

"Well, prolly not ever thang," Pick said. "He prolly didn't know we set a trap for his ass."

"Penis is supposed to help us free Earth," Jack said, confused as shit.

Pick and Rang-er chuckled, sipped their beers and glanced up at Peen-Iz hovering in the air.

Me and Fanger made eye contact and shook our

heads. We was both lost. The only thing I was sure about right at that moment was that we needed that patrol ship. Without it we didn't stand a chance of ever getting back home.

I took a step towards Pick, looked him dead in the eye and said, "We need the ship to get home and save our planet."

Pick nodded, side stepped over to Rang-er and the two of them huddled. They sipped beers, burped and whispered for several minutes before turning back around.

"We like you fellers. We're gonna have a drankin' contest." Pick tossed an empty beer can over me and Fanger and in to the bed of the trank. "Winner gits the ship."

Me and Fanger grinned at each other. Can't nobody out drank Fanger. It didn't matter what planet they came from.

"Hell yeah we can have drankin' contest," I said.

Pick and Rang-er pulled their pistol-like weapons off their hips and fired off five shots each in the air. Ever purple-neck that heard the gunshots hooted and hollered. Them sumbitches all scampered around, climbing down off the mountain and hopping in to vehicles. The tranks revved loud as shit, kicked up dust and lined up along the edge of the clearing.

Down below in the forest a couple of tranks plowed down the trees and shrubs to create another little clearing. Once the trees was all cleared away, four purple-necks dropped outa the bigger of the two tranks, set up two tables in the middle of the clearing and stacked cases of beer on top of the tables. I reckoned five shots in the air musta been the signal for a drinking contest.

"Game's ready," Pick said, pointing down at the clearing below.

I slapped Fanger on the right shoulder with my left hand and said, "Give'em hell!"

"Naw, that ain't how the game works." Pick sipped his beer and looked serious as shit. "You git to choose who dranks on our side and we git to choose who dranks on your side. Y'all choose first."

Me and Fanger turned to each other and lifted our shoulders. Rules was rules. Wasn't no sense in winning a dranking game if you had to break the rules to do it.

I scanned the crowd of purple-necks and spotted a skinny little feller with wide plaid patterns on his face sitting on the back of one of the smaller tranks sipping his beer with little baby sips. I glanced over at Fanger and he gave me a nod. I pointed and said, "That skinny feller right there."

"That'll work." Rang-er pointed at Jack. "And we choose your skinny feller."

I slapped Jack's left shoulder with my right hand and said, "Give'em hell!"

Jack shifted his eyes between me, Fanger, Pick and Rang-er, still confused by ever thang. "A'ight," he said, straightening his arm and handing me the black box controlling Peen-Iz. "Might as well git drunk as shit."

Pick stretched his left arm back and pointed, directing Jack towards one of the tranks. Me and Fanger watched as Jack climbed up in to the back of the vehicle and sat down across from the skinny purple-neck feller. For some reason my belly twitched and I felt kinda like I was sending Jack off to his first day of school.

But that didn't last long. The trank with Jack in it thundered and took off, snapping me be back in to the moment. Somehow I didn't notice that Rang-er had moved right up next to me.

"I'll take that for the time bein'." Rang-er pointed at the black box with his pokey rang fanger. Not sure what else to do, I slapped the black box in his right palm.

Rang-er chuckled and held the black box like a flashlight over his head, spinning Peen-Iz in tight circles. With his left hand, he pulled what appeared to be a roll of purple duct tape outa the back pocket of his his jean shorts and bit on the end of it with his mouth. Twisting his neck, he ripped off a big strip and taped the black box to the bed of a trank parked next to Pick's ride. Peen-Iz hovered in the air like a stiff flag over the vehicle.

Me and Fanger bounced our eyebrows at each other, reached our arms up high, hooked our hands on to tailgate of Pick's trank and hoisted ourselves up. By the time we was standing, Jack was climbing out of the trank down on the smaller clearing.

"Y'all wanna use your weapons or some of ours?" Pick looked up at us from the ground.

I scrunched up my face and said, "For what?"

"For shootin' at the players. What the hell else fer?" Pick shook his head and looked over at Rang-er standing on his right.

"We'll use yours I reckon." Fanger tapped his right fanger on his pistol. "We ain't got much ammo."

A big ass duffle bag flopped in to the bed of the trank. Fanger dropped down on his left knee, unzipped the bag and looked up at me with a big ass smirk.

"Just like home," I said, bending over the top of the duffle bag. I twisted my right hip back and peeked over the side of the bed. "We trying to kill the players or what, Pick?"

"Naw." Pick looked through the scope of his riffle-like weapon. "Just shoot the cans outa their hands to keep'em from drankin'."

"What if a player gits shot?" I stood up straight and looked down at the clearing.

"They git back up and keep drankin'." Rang-er stood next to Pick looking through the scope of his weapon too.

Fanger chuckled to himself as he dug all around in the duffle bag.

"Here's the thang," I said, watching Jack talk to a purple-neck. "We ain't like y'all. If Jack gits shot he dies. He can't git back up."

"Then tell him not to git hit." Pick twisted a dial on the scope of his riffle. He didn't seem all that concerned about shit.

I looked back down at the clearing and spotted Jack still talking to the purple-neck. After a couple of seconds his eyes shot wide open and he jerked his head around, looking up hill for me and Fanger.

"Don't git hit, Jack!" I hollered, hoping to make him feel a little better.

"Good thang for him he's skinny as shit." Fanger stood straight, arms bent and palms up, bouncing a riffle in both his hands.

Pick walked to the edge of the clearing just before it dropped off in to the woods. Without saying a word he held his pistol in the air, squeezed the trigger and fired off one single shot.

The skinny purple-neck feller grabbed a can of beer off the table and chugged it down. Jack bent forward to grab a can and shots rang out from ever direction. Beer cans exploded and beer sprayed all over Jack's face and body.

"Start shootin'!" Pick hollered to me and Fanger.

From the bed of trank, we both laid across the roof of the cab, each of us holding one of them alien purple-neck riffles. I shifted my hips and leaned towards the scope. Before my hand even touched the trigger Fanger was popping off rounds.

Jack, still stunned by the first round of beer can explosions, stood rigid as shit watching his opponent. Ever time that purple sumbitch placed a hand on a can of beer Fanger's riffle fired and blew up a cloud of beer mist right in front of that feller.

I squeezed off a few rounds to git a feel for the alien riffle. But Fanger was firing with his usual precision and accuracy so I just sat my riffle down, cracked open a cold one and enjoyed the show. Jack needed a nudge in the right direction so I hollered, "Drank, Jack! Drank!"

Jack musta worked up a strategy while he was standing there stunned as shit. Soon as I hollered he hooked his hands under the table, lifted with his back and shoulders and flipped the table on its side, tossing ever can of beer on to the ground. Without hesitation—he learned that from being around me and Fanger—he dove over the table and in to the pile of beer cans. Tucking his right shoulder, he rolled over on to his back and laid out flat.

At first I couldn't figure out what the hell was happening. All the purple-necks aimed their weapons, itching to get a shot off, but Jack didn't touch a single beer. Then, like somebody flipped a switch, Jack started tossing beers straight up in the air over his body, bending only his arms like he was one of them toy marching soldiers or a tipped over robot.

Gunshots cracked all around like the Fourth of July, bullets zipped, whizzed and whistled through the air and beer cans exploded in rapid succession. In the middle of it all, Jack laid there sprawled out flat against the ground with his mouth open and eyes closed as beer rained down over his whole body.

"He's a damn genius." I looked over at Fanger and he pulled his head away from his scope long enough to flash a smile.

The purple-necks hooted and hollered, raising hell and enjoying the show. After only a couple minutes, Jack was soaked from head to toe like he'd been swimming in beer and the skinny purple-neck hadn't hardly got a sip in between Fanger's shots.

"Hey Pick!" I hollered. "How do we know who the winner is?"

"First one to pass out wins!" Pick hollered back without looking at me.

Jack stuck his hands in the air, turned them from side to side to show they was empty, kicked his feet up and lifted his shoulders off the ground. In a wobbly motion he rolled up to his feet and stumbled, stretching his lanky arms out to the side for balance.

I tilted my head to Fanger and said, "You thank he knows he wins if he passes out?"

"Maybe," Fanger said, popping off a round.

Jack's head bobbled and he staggered around in a circle, fighting to keep his balance. After a couple of near falls, he bent over and reached for a can of beer. Soon as his fangers touched the can a bullet zinged in and exploded the beer in his face. Squinting to see, he lifted his right foot to step towards another beer.

As his foot hit the ground he lost his balance and fell forward, grazing his head on the side of table and passing out cold.

Two purple-necks hustled in from outa the woods and hunkered down next to Jack. After slapping his face and poking him with sticks, one of the purple fellers stood up straight, raised his right arm in the air and gave the crowd a thumbs up.

"Did Jack win?" Fanger said, pulling his head back and letting his riffle drop to the right.

"Shit yeah!" Pick hollered, holding his pistol over his head. He fired of one shot and the crowd went wild.

I slapped Fanger's shoulder and said, "Jack learned that kinda strategizing from us for damn sure."

Pick and Rang-er walked over to the trank and looked up at me and Fanger.

"Y'all win." Pick said. "Y'all git the ship."

"We got one problem." I pointed down to the clearing. "That's our pilot. We need him to fly the ship."

"Well shit. Come to our party. Git drunk with us." Pick sipped his beer and smiled up at me and Fanger.

Sure as shit we took him up on his offer. Me and

Fanger drank all night long with the purple-necks, shooting alien weapons and dranking alien booze, and Jack played some kinda video games with the skinny purple feller he competed against. As the night progressed, all three of us figured we could live just fine on Fla'Nel if we had to. In fact, we had the most fun we'd had since we fell under attack back home. We even made a deal not to say shit about the invasion or Peen-Iz until the next morning. It felt good as hell to finally have a break from ever thang.

The sun came up and me and Fanger sat on the back of Pick's trank, dangling our feet and sipping our beers while Jack snored loud as shit stretched out behind us in the bed of the vehicle. Peen-Iz, still froze up stiff from the paralyzer black box thang, floated above a trank parked on the other side of the trailer park. A few purple-necks lingered outside—dranking, shooting and raising hell—but most of them had disappeared inside the trailers. Back behind one of the double-wides, Pick and Rang-er filled jars from a moonshine still and loaded them in to crates.

"So what's our strategy?" I said, staring up at the purple sunrise.

"I reckon we need Penis." Fanger scratched his

head and sniffed. "Even if we can't trust his ass. He knows shit we don't."

I chewed on my bottom lip, pissed off that Fanger was right. Without Peen-Iz we didn't have a clue how to fight them buncha dumb, stankin', worthless asshole sumbitches. "We're gonna have to convince the purple-necks to let Penis come with us."

"Yep," Fanger said, nodding towards Pick and Rang-er as they headed towards us.

"You fellers are all set." Pick pointed back with his right thumb. "We'll git them crates loaded on your ship."

Me and Fanger swung our legs, hopped our butts off the tailgate and bounced down to the ground.

"We need Penis." I figured it was best to get straight to business. "He's the only one who can show us how to save our planet. Even if he is a backstabbing, double-crossing, two-timing asshole."

"He don't give a shit about y'all or your planet." Pick crossed his arms and shook his head. "Them Bom'Kyn sumbitches inserted him in to your team just to screw y'all over. They do that kinda shit."

"We ain't got no choice." Fanger looked Rang-er dead in the eye.

"What do Penis and the Bom'Kynians want from y'all?" Pick shifted his eyes between me and Fanger.

"Penis wants this here invisibility device I been totin' around." I slapped my overall bib pocket with my right hand.

"We already knew that shit," Rang-er chuckled. "That was our Penis bait."

"Yeah, we was purty sure you didn't have one giant boob on your chest." Pick slapped Rang-er's shoulder and grinned. "We figured y'all would tell us about it sooner or later. Y'all was just doin' what me and Rang-er woulda done."

I pressed my lips together and nodded, knowing me and Fanger would have given our double-gangers the same chance to come clean.

"The Bom'Kynians want our whoop ass device," Fanger said. He didn't care much for bonding and shit.

"Y'all got a whoop ass device?" Rang-er glanced at Pick and back to me and Fanger.

"Maybe." Fanger sipped his beer.

"We thank we do if we can find it." I stared at Pick and Rang-er, trying to get a read on what they was thinking.

Pick and Rang-er stared back at me and Fanger. Probably doing the same damn thing.

After several seconds of ever body trying to figure each other out, Pick uncrossed his arms and said, "We know you fellers are just now learnin' about space and Bom'Kynians and all that shit. There's a shit ton y'all don't know."

"More than a shit ton," Rang-er said, nodding along with Pick.

"Bom'Kynians don't just steal shit." Pick turned between me and Fanger. "They wipe out planets completely. They're dumb as shit but powerful 'cause of all the technology they stole."

Me and Fanger nodded along too, trying to keep Pick talking.

"A big war is brewing." Pick's voice got even more serious. "All the planets that hate the Bom'Kynians are starting to team up. The problem is some of the teams don't like each other neither. It's a big ass mess."

"More than a big ass mess," Rang-er said.

"So far Fla'Nel has stayed out of it." Pick looked away then back at me and Fanger. "But that won't last. And we're one of the weaker planets when it comes to technology."

I glanced over at Fanger. From the look on his face he was hoping this was going were I was hoping it was going.

Pick lifted his feet, adjusted his stance and said, "If y'all got a whoop ass device, sumpin' that can help protect our planet, we need to team up. We need all the technology we can git."

"We'll shit yeah," I said, standing up straight. "Let's do this shit."

"Yep, let's do this shit." Fanger hoked pokey fangers with Rang-er.

"Hey fellers." Jack sat up in the bed of the trank, squinting his eyes and rubbing his head. "What the hell is going on?"

"We're teaming up with the purple-necks!" I hollered, grinning big as shit. "Pick and Rang-er are coming to Earth with us to find our whoop ass device and help keep Penis under control."

"Shit yeah!" Pick and Rang-er hollered.

Jack fell backwards and passed out again in the bed of the trank. Me, Fanger, Pick and Rang-er decided it was best to have one more party before heading off for Earth. We figured a good buzz would give us a boost on our strategizing. So we ignored Peen-Iz, drank shit loads and worked ourselves up to whoop them buncha dumb, stankin', worthless asshole sumbitches' asses good and run them off our planet.

THE DEVICE

BOOK 6

DEPARTURE_

THE MORE TIME ME, Fanger and Jack spent with Pick, Rang-er and the other Purple-Necks the more our similarities stood out. After our one more night of dranking we decided to have another one more night of dranking just to get ready to whoop ass back home. We drank, shot weapons, loaded the ship full of space beer and space moonshine. We even set up a still like we used to have on the MTRV. We stocked the patrol ship with ever thang we needed to live out in space for months. That shit was set to go.

Our biggest problem was how to deal with Peen-Iz. That sumbitch had been locked up stiff for days, hovering in the air over different tranks and shit like one of them parade balloons. Me, Fanger and Jack didn't trust him for shit but we needed his help. We had no doubt he would stab us in the back again given the chance. But there wasn't a chance in Hell he was gonna help us if he didn't have some freedom.

Pick and Rang-er didn't want Peen-Iz on the mission at all. They was ready just to kill his ass and fight on with out his help. But since we was double gangers and all, they tolerated him.

After lots of dranking, strategizing, role playing scenarios with and without weapons and general conversation, we all came to the conclusion the only option was to set Peen-Iz free to see what he would do. We figured if he was gonna back stab us right away it was best that it happened on Fla'Nel where we had some control rather than out in space or back on Earth where we was vulnerable. If he decided to help us that was the best. If he decided to run off at least we wouldn't be distracted by having to contain his ass.

Another smaller problem was figuring out where the Hell to free that sumbitch. From what we knew about Peen-Iz he was Bom'Kynian. And one thang we knew about Bom'Kynians was they needed that fresh ass air to live. Them sumbitches couldn't just walk around on Earth or Fla'Nel and survive. That little tidbit complicated our decision making. We didn't want that back-stabbing shit head to die just yet but we sure as shit didn't want to have to set him free on the ship.

And just to mix shit up even more, Jack swore up and down that Peen-Iz told him he had trained to breathe any air, not just the fresh ass air for Bom'Kynians.

Pick and Rang-er were fine to release that asshole on the planet and let whatever was gonna happen happen. Me and Fanger wanted to be more strategic but we was running outa time.

"Let's just do this shit," I said, lowering my arm and positioning Peen-Iz with his feet on the purple dirt. I was tired of all the back and forth. I figured Jack was probably right. He knew Peen-Iz better than the rest of us.

We all stood grouped together several feet from the space ship. After one last look around at the other fellers, I clicked the button on the black box and Peen-Iz dropped down to the ground on to is hands and knees.

"Shit, fellers," Peen-Iz said, taking in a deep breath, "I'm surprised y'all let my ass go."

Me, Fanger, Jack, Pick and Rang'er all stood side by side with our hands on our pistols strapped to our right hips. None of us said squat. We just waited and observed. It sure as shit looked like Peen-Iz could breathe the air just fine.

Peen-Iz tilted his head up, stepped his right foot forward and pushed up, dragging his left foot up beside his right foot. Shaking out his hands and arms, he grinned and said, "What's the plan?"

Peen-Iz was damn good at the unexpected. All our practice scenarios were based on Peen-Iz being pissed as shit. We never suspected he would act like he was part of the team.

"That sumbitch is working a plan," Rang-er said, tapping his pistol with his pokey fanger.

"Damn sure is." Fanger nodded and wrapped his fangers around his pistol, ready to draw.

Me and Pick looked at each other for a second then I turned to Peen-Iz and said, "We know we can't trust your ass. We know you're gonna stab us in the back again. But we're gonna let you help until it don't make sense no more."

Peen-Iz sniffed, wiped his nose with the back of his right hand and shifted his eyes between the five of us. "Let's connect the invisibility device to the ship. We can sneak back to Earth and git y'all's whoop ass device. That work for y'all?"

"Yep," well all said at the same time, knowing plain as shit Peen-Iz just made it clear he was after the whoop ass device. We could most likely expect his help at least until we had the device in our possession.

Me and Fanger escorted Pick and Rang-er up the ramp and onto our ship. Peen-Iz and Jack followed behind, chattering away like a couple teenagers gossiping in the school hallway.

"Kinda plain in here, ain't it?" Pick said, scanning the the inside of the ship as he stepped inside.

"Yep," I said. "But there's more than meets the eye."

"That the crew?" Rang-er pointed to the clear ball on the ceiling with the crew frozen inside.

"Yep," Fanger said, sipping his beer.

I pulled the invisibility device outa my overall bib pocket with my left hand, twisted to the left and tossed the device back to Jack.

Jack stretched his arms forward, squatted down backwards in an awkward position, and fumbled the device between his hands, damn near dropping it on the floor before hugging it tight against his chest. Watching that shit you would never suspect Jack was any good in a fight.

Peen-Iz waved his right arm in the air and Jack fell in behind. The two of them hauled ass over to the control panel and slid to a stop in unison like they was in the Ice Capades. Jack hunched over and watched ever move Peen-Iz made as he swiped and tapped away.

The back wall of the ship swirled and a hallway appeared.

"More than meets the eye," Pick said, nudging Rang-er in the shoulder.

Peen-Iz and Jack took off down the hallway, talking to themselves like they was best friends. Jack even let out a couple giggles before they disappeared out of earshot.

Me, Fanger, Pick and Rang-er cracked opened beers and sipped in silence. Before we could finish, Peen-Iz and Jack walked fast as shit back towards us.

"Git back," Peen-Iz said, eyeballing Pick as he moved in to position behind the control panel. He tapped the controls and said, "Ship's invisible. Where to?"

"Where we goin' first?" Jack took position next to Peen-Iz and tapped the controls too.

"Earth. Take us in to orbit, I reckon," I said with a half shrug. Peen-Iz working with us so easily took me off guard. The uncertainty was almost causing me to hesitate. Almost.

Peen-Iz gave a nod and lifted his right hand toward the control panel. But before his stubby ass fangers touched the panel a loud ass sound like a mix between a poot and a fog horn blasted from outside.

"Wait, fellers!" Pick said, locking eyes with Rang-er.

"What the hell is that noise?" I shot glances between Fanger and Jack and our two double gangers. From the corner of my eye I saw Peen-Iz step away from the control panel, stroking his beard and glancing around.

"That's the alarm," Pick said, "our planet's about to be under attack." He looked at Rang-er and shook his head.

"We gotta help," Rang-er said, tapping his right hand on his hip.

Me, Fanger and Jack all said, "A'ight." The three of us understood the situation they was facing.

Pick and Rang-er spun around, looking for the damn exit.

"Jack, lower the door," I said, pointing Pick and Rang-er in the right direction.

"Light suits, weapons and shit." Fanger tossed his beer can to the side with that shit still half full. Fanger don't never was no beer. That ole boy meant business and he was always, always thanking.

Jack tapped the control panel and the walls swirled open in to the weapons room.

"One of ever thang," Peen-Iz hollered, hustling over to the weapons room.

Peen-Iz being so helpful really wasn't much help at all. It put the rest of us on edge but what could we do. I waved the others in to the weapons room and we hustled in behind Peen-Iz. By the time we got there Peen-Iz had a whole damn duffle bag full of gear.

"What the hell is in here?" Pick said, stretching out his right arm towards Peen-Iz.

"All kinda shit." Peen-Iz released the handle in to Pick's hand. "Test it all out by pointing at the mountain or some shit. Push the buttons on top and see what they do. Even the dumbest Bom'Kynians can use them."

"Light suits!" Jack spun on his right heel, hauled ass back to the control panel and started tapping away. The wall on the other side of the ship swirled open to the locker room.

I nudged Pick and Fanger nudged Rang-er outa the weapons room. The four of us sprinted past Jack and the control panel and in to the locker room.

"Find one that fits," I said, pulling suits out one by one and sizing them up. "Matter of fact, take extras for some of the other fellas. Just leave us a few."

Fanger grabbed a duffle bag from a locker with his left hand, let it dangle open, and ran along the lockers, stuffing as many light suits in as he could with his right hand.

"Preciate it, fellers," Pick said.

"Damn straight." Rang-er bounced his right leg and twitched his mouth from side to side. That sun of a gun was itching to get on the planet to help his buddies fight whoever the hell was about to attack.

"Doors open! Ramps down!" Jack hollered.

Me, Fanger, Pick and Rang-er all glanced around at each other for a second or two. None of us was really the long good bye types.

Pick and Rang-er nodded one more time then sprinted toward the ramp, both totin' big ass duffle bags.

"We'll come back just as soon as we free Earth," I hollered.

"Give'em hell!" Fanger hollered even louder.

Pick and Rang-er hopped off the ramp to the purple dirt below. Soon as the ramp started to close an explosion blasted in the distant. More and more explosions followed, getting closer to us with each blast.

"Our ship's still invisible!" Jack hollered. "What's the plan?"

"Run," Peen-Iz said, with a the most serious look I ever seen on that sumbitch's face.

"How many ships, Jack?" I kept my eyes locked on Peen-Iz.

"Looks like ten!" Jack hollered, starring down at the control panel with Peen-Iz on his right.

"Skoalarians," Peen-Iz said, "they run in packs of ten."

"Skoalarian? Skoalarian?" I repeated the name and processed it in my head. "They don't sound so bad."

"Yeah, I think I might like to meet them," Fanger said, crossing his arms and staring at Peen-Iz

"Shit," Peen-Iz mumbled, tugging on his beard and shifting his eyes between me and Fanger. He knew he was gonna have to tell us more about the Skoalarians. And sure as shit he started talking, "Purple-necks and Skoalarians used to be allies. Then one day a while back sumpin' mighta happened that caused them two to hate each other. The cause of that sumpin' might have been me following orders to put a wedge between'em. Y'all happy now that I told ya?"

"No," me, Fanger and Jack all said at the same time.

"So, how did you cause the Purple-necks and

Skoalarins to hate each other?" I said, with one hundred percent true curiosity.

Peen-Iz let out a sigh, "I stole shit from one, planted it with the other. Getting people pissed off at each other is easy to do. Let's just get back to the mission."

I titled my head to the right and stared at Peen-Iz. I was purty sure he really was showing some kinda regret for his past. And for a split second I had a gut feeling that maybe some day we would be able to trust Peen-Iz. But this wasn't the day. People don't change easy no matter what planet they're from.

"Can the Purple-necks fight off the Skolarians?" I hustled over to the control panel.

"Maybe." Peen-Iz bumped Jack with his left shoulder and pushed his way in front of the control panel. He didn't say shit. Just tapped away like a maniac.

"Say sumpin', Penis," Fanger said, without even the slightest chuckle.

The explosions stopped just as fast as they started. I stepped closer to the control panel and watched Peen-Iz's fangers slip and slide across the screen.

"More ships headed this way," Peen-Iz said.

"Is that good or bad?" I said.

Peen-Iz ignored me and worked the controls.

I bent forward with my head over the control panel and wrenched my neck up to look Peen-Iz in the eye. "Whats goin' on, dammit?"

"I can't say for sure," Peen-Iz said, kinda talking to himself.

Jack stretched his neck over the top of Peen-Iz, stared down at the screen and said, "A shit ton of ships are coming."

"What are they doin'?" Fanger said through a sip of beer.

"It kinda looks like they're gettin' ready to fight the Skoalarians, I think." Jack rolled back on to his heels.

The explosions picked up again. Jack was right. I could see on the screen the approaching ships were firing on the Skoalarians.

"We better git the hell outa here if y'all wanna save your planet." Peen-Iz stood up straight and crossed his arms.

"Let's take out some of the Skoalarian ships," I said, looking between Fanger and Jack. "It looks like them other ships are here to help Fla'Nel. Let's help some too, fellers."

"Shit yeah," Fanger and Jack said without a damn second of hesitation.

"Arm the weapons or whatever the hell you're supposed to say, Penis." I couldn't resist a little chuckle. Fanger and Jack cracked smiles too. The prospect of battle was lifting our spirits some.

Peen-Iz stretched his arms in the air and shook his head, knowing we wasn't gonna leave with out kicking a little alien ass on the way out. His chubby fangers tapped on the control panel and an alarm sounded. "Weapons loaded. But I'll warn you. We ain't got much fire power in this here patrol ship. We really should save it for Earth."

"These weapons ain't gonna do shit anyway to stop the invasion. Might as well make use of them now," I said.

"Damn right," Fanger said.

"Can we fire while we're invisible?" Jack asked, dampening the damn mood a little.

"Shit yeah." Peen-Iz looked confused as shit. "Why wouldn't we be able to fire while we're invisible?"

"No reason." Jack waved his right hand in he air. "Guess I watch too much TV or some shit."

"Penis, I know you know some kinda strategy for firing on enemy ships," I said. "Start doing that shit."

I could tell Peen-Iz really hated taking orders from me. I could also tell he was just tolerating it to get what he wanted for his endgame. But for the time being I decided to have some fun with it.

"Fanger, you got any orders for Penis?" I said.

"Not yet but I will." Fanger grinned and cracked open a fresh beer, staring at Peen-Iz the whole time.

"When you're invisible," Peen-Iz said, not really paying us no attention, " the best strategy is to attack and move. It confuses the shit outa the enemy. So where gonna fire on the closest ship, shoot up in to orbit, drop down in another location and fire on the next ship we see. We'll repeat that a few times until we take one or maybe two out. Sound like a plan fellers?"

Peen-Iz sure a shit reverted back into his talky ass self. Must be on of them defense mechanisms I used to hear my court-ordered therapist talk about.

"Sounds good to me," I said, looking between Fanger and Jack. The two of them just shrugged and sipped beer.

A TV screen appeared on the wall across from us and the ship whirred. In a flash we was face to face with one of them Skoalarian ships. To my surprise, well kinda, the ship looked like a flying can of dip.

"Makes sense," I heard Fanger say.

Our ship jolted and a ball of light shot out

towards the enemy vessel. Just as an explosion appeared on the screen our ship whirred. I saw Fla'Nel from space appear on the screen and the ship whirred again. In another flash we was face to face with another Skoalarian ship.

The same shit happened again. A light ball fired, explosion starts on the TV and the ship whirs again. The process was starting to make me dizzy as shit so I sipped my beer faster to compensate.

"Two's enough," Peen-Iz said, turning his head up from the control panel. "Them other sumbitches can handle the rest."

"So who are they? They ones helpin' Fla'Nel?" Jack asked.

"Can't say," Peen-Iz said in a low voice.

Sumpin' told me that sumbitch probably knew but it wasn't worth forcing it outa him. We needed to keep on mission.

Me, Fanger and Jack moved together in front of the control panel and watched the TV screen as the other squadron took out the Skoalarians.

"Pick and Rang-er told us," I said, "There's a war coming."

"Yep." Fanger nodded, keeping his eyes on the TV.

"What's the plan, Lick?" Jack said, backing away and taking position at the control panel.

"Earth. Take us in to orbit," I said. "We'll join this fight once we run them sumbitches off our planet."

Peen-Iz let out a sigh and mumbled, "Finally."

I looked over at Fanger with my eyebrows all scrunched up like I smelled a fart. We was gonna have to figure out how to handle Peen-Iz. My ears tingled, taking my mind off dealing with Peen-Iz for the time being, and a TV screen flashed up on the wall.

"Ho. Lee. Shit," me, Fanger and Jack said at the same damn time.

WE ALL STARED at the TV screen on the wall with our jaws dangling wide open. Except for Peen-Iz, that is. That asshole was used to seeing invasions and shit. He just stood there scratching his head and looking at me, Fanger and Jack like we was specimens he couldn't quite figure out.

We couldn't hardly tell we was orbiting Earth. Space ships of all sizes surrounded the planet, purty much blocking the view of the surface below. The best I could tell there was more ships, and I mean a shitload more, than there were the last time when Peen-Iz brought us here.

"That shit ain't good," Fanger said, shaking his head and twisting his mouth.

"Ho. Lee. Shit." Jack stared at the TV. "Ships and mini golf courses."

"What about people?" I stepped closer to the screen.

Jack bent over and danced his fangers over the controls and after a second said, "Can't say."

"They're in storage." Peen-Iz pulled on his beard, looked at me, Fanger and Jack, and pointed up to the ceiling. "Kinda like the crew."

"Why the hell they storin' people?" I crossed my arms and locked my eyes on Peen-Iz.

"It's the process," Peen-Iz said. "First the planet inhabitants get put in two groups. Ones they can clone go in one group and ones they can't clone get put in another. The clone ones get sent to Bom'Kyn right away like your friends. They start the cloning process fast as shit. The others go to storage until they need'em."

"What happens to the ones they can't clone?" Jack asked.

"They get brainwashed and used for whatever." Peen-Iz pulled his beard out real long and held the tip.

"Whatever? What's whatever?" I said.

"Soldiers. Decoys. Shit like that." Peen-Iz almost looked like he gave a shit about them. "Good news is all the people they can't clone are prolly still on the planet. Moving them to permanent storage is the last step. Right now they're doing a sweep and looking for technology to steal. That step usually takes a while. Once the ships leave the planet it's pretty much depleted."

"We need to get the whoop ass device." Fanger crushed his beer can with his right hand, pokey fanger out. "It's time to run these sumbitches off our planet."

"Where is the whoop ass device?" Peen-Iz said, all casual like we was having tea together or some shit.

"We got a couple places to look. We'll find it." I bobbed my head slow and sipped my beer.

Peen-Iz darted his eyes between me and Fanger and blurted out, "Y'all don't know where it is?"

"We know where it ain't," Fanger said.

"What the hell does that mean?" Peen-Iz let his jaw drop open and dangle.

"Means we know it ain't in the junkyard," I said. "And if it ain't there that narrows it down."

"Where should I go, Lick?" Jack leaned forward and rested both hands on the edge of control panel.

"Bunker?" I said to Fanger.

"Bunker," Fanger said with a nod.

"Where the hell is the bunker?" Jack said. "Y'all never told me about that shit."

"Never needed to." Fanger sipped his beer and winked his left eye at me.

"The bunker is under our trailer," I said. "We stored our experimental projects there. We stopped using it a while back. Most of the shit in there we forgot about. It's possible if we was working on the whoop ass device, and it kinda worked a little, we mighta put it in the bunker."

Jack tilted his head to the left and scratched his right temple with his right middle fanger. "How the hell did y'all forget about weapons y'all was building?"

"Seddy," Fanger said with a half grin.

"For that last year or so we been stayin' at the junkyard and talkin' into seddy ever night." I chugged a big swoller of beer and continued, "Any new weapons and shit we thought up we just kept at the junkyard. The older ones we just stopped tinekerin' with. Seddy purty much consumed us, I reckon."

"Makes sense," Jack said, sucking his bottom lip in to his mouth and glancing between me and Fanger.

Peen-Iz arched his eyebrows real big and spun

his right hand in circle to try and speed thangs along. "So where's the trailer with the bunker underneath it?"

"It's on the south side of the sewage treatment plant," I said. "Head that way and I'll show you where to go."

Peen-Iz nodded at Jack and pointed to the control panel, giving Jack the go ahead to control the ship.

Jacked tapped the controls while the rest of us watched the TV screen. A tiny little tingle tickled my ears as the ship sank outa orbit and we floated along the surface of the planet just over the tree line. Jack was right as shit. All I could see was ships and mini golf courses for miles and miles.

"That's it." I pointed to the TV. "That's the sewage treatment plant. Our trailer is in that patch of woods just to the south."

Jack raised his right thumb at me without looking up from the controls.

The image on the TV screen spun around until we was looking straight down at the top of the double wide trailer me and Fanger bought together years ago.

"Take us down between the sewage treatment plant and the woods," I told Jack.

This is where I figured it was gonna get tricky. We had to figure out just how to handle Peen-Iz. That sumbitch was likely to steal the whoop ass device the damn second we had it in our possession.

Me and Fanger had discussed freezing Peen-Iz up again while we fetched the whoop ass device, but we figured that would just piss him off and ruin his cooperation. Whatever we did we was gonna have to do with Peen-Iz still in full motion. One thing I knew for sure is that me, Fanger and Jack, to some degree, was getting purty damn tired of dancing around trying to predict what the hell Peen-Iz was up to.

"You're gonna behave, right Penis?" I said.

"Yeah, no dickin' around, right Penis?" Fanger said, with a grin.

Me and Jack couldn't help letting out a few chuckles.

"I'm with you fellers," Peen-z said with a serious ass look on his face.

"A'ight." I stared at Peen-Iz hoping he would give something away. But that sumbitch was too good at deception to read. "Me, Fanger and Penis will recover the whoop ass device. Jack, you man the ship. Operation Recover Shit Bater Twelve underway."

Taking Peen-Iz with me and Fanger was a calculated risk. No damn way was we gonna leave his ass on the ship alone with Jack. Just in case, I had the black box freezey thang on my left hip ready to draw and freeze his ass up again in an emergency.

"Lower the ramp, Jack." I pivoted on my right heel to face Fanger. The two of us hooked our thumbs in our overall straps to activate our light suits.

"Don't do that shit!" Peen-Iz hollered. "Turn them on and the bigguns will know we're here. They can detect the light suits."

Me and Fanger just shrugged it off. If we was gonna have to fight alien critters without light suits this was the place to do it. We was comfortable as shit on our home turf.

I pivoted again on my right heel, raised my right arm and hustled down the ramp. At the bottom I clinched my right fist, stopping Fanger and Peen-Iz in their tracks, and rotated my head from left to right, scanning the area. No Bill Cooper and Maybelle Turner critters and no other alien assholes anywhere in sight. No ships in the area either.

Taking the lead, I bent my knees and hopped forward and off the ramp. I dropped down about three feet and bent my knees again to cushion the landing. It felt good to be standing on Earth again. If

I was the emotional type I mighta even gotten a little tear in my eye. But I ain't so I didn't.

Fanger and Peen-Iz hit the ground right behind me. All three of us scanned the area for any critters, aliens or some other kinda shit we might not have thought up. I raised my right arm, waved it towards the trailer and we all broke into a sprint.

Me and Fanger never got around to installing any underpinning so under the trailer was wide ass open. Without slowing down, I leaned to right, dropped down on my right hip and slid under the trailer. With a quick ass roll, I flopped over on my belly, rested with my elbows on the ground and scanned the area again as Fanger and Peen-Iz slide under the trailer beside me.

After a quick nod to the fellers, I scuttled backwards on me knees and elbows to the center of the trailer. I glanced up and found the hatch me and Fanger cut into the trailer floor to access the bunker from inside the trailer. Directly below the hatch I dug my right hand in to the dirt and dust that had settled and patted around for the handle.

Fanger took position across from me and swiped his right arm over the ground in a big arch to brush the dirt and dust away, exposing the bunker hatch door.

Peen-Iz stayed back a few feet, watching with a blank ass look on his face. No telling what that sumbitch was thinking.

Once I had a tight grip on the handle, I pulled up and twisted the handle to the right in one motion. As I lifted the hatch, lights flickered on below us. Me and Fanger rigged it so the lights would turn on automatically.

I scooted around in a circle on my belly, let me feet dangle down into the hatch and found my footing on the access ladder. I stepped down a few steps until I could grab the sides of the ladder with both hands. With a slight hop, I hooked me feet on the the sides of the ladder then let the ladder slide through my hands as I dropped down into the bunker. Me and Fanger trained to enter the bunker fast as shit. It had been a while but I still had the muscle memory to execute the maneuver.

Without looking back, I hustled over to the the safe door me and Fanger rigged as the access to the main room of the bunker. As I nestled up to the door with my left shoulder, I heard Fanger and then Peen-Iz hit the ground behind me. With my right fangers, I spun the combination lock fast as shit. I pulled it open with both hands and it unsealed with a hiss.

The bunker lights flickered and I stepped

through the doorway. The slightly stale ass air felt like home sweet home. My eyes darted left and right, taking in the cases of beer, jars of moonshine and bottles of whiskey stacked from the floor to ceiling. "Ready as shit," I mumbled to myself.

"Trained as shit too," Fanger said right over my shoulder.

"Hot damn, fellers," Peen-Iz said as he stepped inside.

"You ain't seen nothing yet." Fanger stretched his right arm and grabbed a whiskey bottle off one of the shelves.

I cracked open a beer, looked Peen-Iz in the eye and twitched my head towards the back of the bunker.

Peen-Iz turned sideways and scuttled past Fanger, ducking under the whiskey bottle Fanger had pressed to his lips and tilted up to the ceiling.

I moseyed to the back of the bunker, taking just a minute for myself to enjoy the taste of Earth beer. I finished off my last swoller and set my empty beer can on the shelf to my right. Opening and closing my hands and stretching my fangers out, I approached the safe door that led to the weapons room. Without looking back, I spun out the combination with my right fangers.

"Let's see what we got," I said as I leaned back and pulled the door open with both hands.

Lights clicked on and the weapons room lit up bright as shit.

"Holy shit, fellers." Peen-Iz shuffled past me and in to the room like he was in a trance.

I stepped through the door and memories of explosions and visits to the emergency room flashed through my mind. The good ole days. My eyes wandered from shelf to shelf taking in the experimental guns, rockets, explosive devices and other shit I couldn't quite remember exactly.

Fanger walked up beside me, pointing to the back wall with his pokey fanger and said, "I remember now."

Sitting on the very back shelf sat something that was outa place compared to the other weapons and shit in the room. An old, black stereo receiver from one of them big ass stereos everybody had in the 80s and 90s stood out among the hand held weapons and ammo on the shelves around it..

"That's it," I said, smiling a little.

"Yep," Fanger said.

"That's the whoop ass device?" Peen-Iz scratched his head.

I stepped to the shelf, stretched out both arms and picked up the device with both hands.

Peen-Iz moved up real close to me, bent over a little and peeked in through the vents on the device. "How does that thang work?"

"Vibration," Fanger said, twisting the lid on his bottle of whiskey.

"Me and Fanger saw a show on vibration," I said. "We learned ever thang in the universe vibrates. Vibration is the soul of the universe."

"Hold up." Peen-Iz stood straight and threw his right hand in the air. "Say that again."

"Vibration is the soul of the universe," I said.

"It can be a force of beauty or a force of destruction," Fanger said right after me, almost like we had rehearsed or some shit.

"Focus and control vibration and you control the universe," Peen-Iz said fast as shit. He slapped his forehead with his left hand and dropped his head down towards the floor.

I glanced over and Fanger and back at Peen-Iz. "Did you see the show too?"

"You fellers sure you made that device?" Peen-Iz rubbed both his hands through his greasy ass hair and shook his head.

"Sure as shit we did." I scrunched up my mouth

and gave Fanger a big nod.

Peen-Iz turned his head to the side, leaned in real close, and put his right eye up against the vent again. His head moved up and down as he peered inside the device. Straightening his back up he said, "You fellers did not make this shit."

"Hell yeah we did." Fanger bowed his back a little and stepped towards Peen-Iz.

"Where did you get the parts?" Peen-Iz crossed his arms and looked between me and Fanger.

"Junkyard." Fanger took a step closer to Peen-Iz. "Where else would we git the shit?"

"How does it work?" Peen-Iz asked.

"Vibration," Fanger said, backing off a little. That ole boy liked to talk science and shit. "It creates vibration waves that destroy shit. The waves our device sends out destroys all the other vibration waves. Ever thang has a vibration so ever thang can be destroyed. "

"It works too." I said. "We'll kinda. We kept blowing out speakers before we could really get it to do anything. But sure as shit the vibrations we sent destroyed shit."

"Yep," Fanger nodded. "We kept it cause we figured if we could get a big enough speaker we could make it work."

"Sound waves?" Peen-Iz said. "This shit works on sound waves?"

"Vibration actually," Fanger said. "Sound waves is what we was using to make the vibration."

Peen-Iz squat down and looked at the device from a distance. After a couple of seconds he stood up straight again and glanced between me and Fanger. His mouth dropped open like he was gonna say some shit but he stopped himself.

Me and Fanger made eye contact and musta been thanking the same damn thang. This was the first time we ever seen Peen-Iz speechless and slightly confused. It was awkward as hell and concerning as shit.

Peen-Iz shook his head really fast, snapping himself outa whatever thought he was in, and said, "Let's just git the device back to the ship. I have an idea."

"Want anything else from hear?" I said to Fanger.

"I got what I need." Fanger held up a small duffle bag filled with whiskey and moonshine.

"Move out!" I hollered, tucking the device in real tight under my right arm. I kept my left hand free to freeze Peen-Iz up if that asshole got outa hand.

Fanger spun on his right heel, tossed the duffle

strap over his right shoulder, and hauled ass through the bunker to the ladder. Peen-Iz fell in behind and I brought up the rear, closing the safe doors as I made my way through the bunker.

Fanger and Peen-Iz we're both up the ladder by the time I made it below the hatch door, "Haul ass," I said, waving them both on with my left hand.

I scurried up the ladder fast as shit one handed, poked my head through the hatch, and scanned the area for any alien sumbitches. I caught a glimpse of Fanger and Peen-Iz standing on the bottom of the ramp. Fanger waved his right hand real big to give me the all clear.

I lurched up through the hatch, rolled over on back, pushed along the ground one foot a time and wiggled side to side out from under the trailer, hugging the device tight as shit against my chest. Soon as I saw the sky, I rolled to left and tucked the whoop ass device under my right arm. Pushing up with my left arm, I hopped forward and pounced up to my feet. I kept my eyes locked on the base of the ramp as I hauled ass for the ship.

Soon as I got within leaping distance, I kicked my left leg up in front of me, pulling my knee damn near to my chest, and pushed off with my right leg.

My left foot then my right landed on the ramp and I hollered, "Close it up, Jack!"

"All clear," Fanger hollered from inside the ship.

The ramp raised to a close behind me, and huffing and puffing to catch my breathe, I wrapped both arms around the device, half way expecting Peen-Iz to pull some shit on me. But that sumbitch didn't do a damn thang. He just gave me nod like he approved of how we executed the mission.

"Where's the device?" Jack said from behind the control panel.

I loosened my hug and raised the device up in front of me.

"That's it?" Jack looked confused as shit.

"Vibration waves, right?" Peen-Iz said, before we could explain shit to Jack. "I have an idea."

Peen-Iz strutted around to the control panel, nudged Jack outa the way with his right shoulder and tapped on the controls. My ears tingled and a shit load of asteroids appeared on the TV screen.

"What the hell are you doin', Peen-Iz," I said. I shifted the device under my right arm and lowered my left hand to the freezey gun thang on my left hip. From the corner of my eye I saw Fanger wrapping his right fangers around his pistol on his right hip.

"Take it easy fellers," Peen-Iz said. "I think I

know a way to test the whoop ass device."

"Explain." Fanger side stepped in front on me, putting himself between me and Peen-Iz.

"You said the device works by using vibration to destroy shit, right?" Peen-Iz kept on talking before anybody could say shit. "The shields on this ship, and all ships really, work by creating vibrations around the ship. I'm thanking instead of the speakers you fellers kept blowing out we could use your device to boost the vibration of the shield. We can test out here on these astroids. What do you fellers thank?"

"I'm a little lost," Jack said, looking at me, Fanger and Peen-Iz.

"We'll explain later," I said, watching Jack's face scrunch up. "Can you connect the device to the ship, Penis?"

"Guess we'll find out." Peen-Iz smiled real big.

Peen-Iz seemed a little too happy for me to relax. I couldn't figure out for shit what the hell was going on with that sumbitch.

"That sumbitch ain't right in the head," Fanger said, leaning in close to me and talking low.

I wrapped my arms around the device again, squeezed it tight in to my chest and said, "One step at a time. Just the way we trained to do."

TEST RUN_

M<small>E AND</small> F<small>ANGER</small> stood glaring at Peen-Iz for what seemed like forever. Peen-Iz stared right back at us with his hands open in front of himself and his shoulders slightly shrugged. Jack just watched the three of us looking at each other with his mouth open and eyebrows raised, confused as shit.

Conflicting urges pulsed through my mind and body. Part of me wanted to launch Peen-Iz out in to space and part of me wanted to really believe he had our best interests in mind. But we didn't have time for soul searching, so I shook off both urges and went in to action mode to keep us moving forward. "Let's just do this shit," I said, breaking the silence.

Peen-Iz clapped his hands, tucked his head down

and tapped the control panel. The walls swirled and the mechanical room appeared at the back of the ship. Peen-Iz clapped again, side stepped around the control panel and took off for the mechanical room.

Me, Fanger and Jack trotted off behind him like three little puppies with me hugging the whoop ass device tight as shit in to my chest. All three of us stutter stepped to a stop like we was line dancing or some shit right outside the mechanical room.

Just inside the room, Peen-Iz rubbed his right hand on one of the big ass cubes that filled the room, grabbed a handle and pulled out a little shelf. He thumped the shelf with his left pointy fanger and said, "Set the device here."

I glanced over at Fanger and he had his left thumb hooked in his light suit strap and his right hand on his pistol, ready for action if shit went sideways.

I loosened my hug on the whoop ass device and let it drop down into my hands. I waited one second, just to see if my gut was gonna tell me something to make me stop, but I didn't feel a damn thang. I walked slow as shit towards the cube, stretched out my arms and sat the device down on the shelf.

Peen-Iz didn't skip a beat. Soon as the device was down that sumbitch tapped with both hands on a little screen on the side of the cube. A tiny blue beam of light blinked on next to the whoop ass device and scanned it all over before disappearing. After a couple more swipes and taps, Peen-Iz stepped back from the cube, rubbed his hands together and said, "We're ready. Let's see what happens."

"That's it?" I said, looking back over my shoulder at Fanger and Jack.

"That's it. Super easy." Peen-Iz smiled from ear to ear, pointed both his pointy fangers towards the control panel and jogged past me, Fanger and Jack.

Jack scurried off right behind him and Fanger took a step closer to me.

"You get the feeling Penis ain't telling us ever thang?" Fanger said real low.

"Ever time that sumbitch talks." I patted Fanger's right shoulder with my left hand and the two of us jogged side by side to the control panel.

Several paces in front of us, Peen-Iz bellied up to the control panel and Jack slid to a stop right next to him. Jack never took his eyes off of Peen-Iz, watching him like a hawk and taking in ever thang he could about the ship. Peen-Iz pointed at the controls and talked fast as shit, explaining how the device worked to Jack.

Jack popped his head up, looked at me and

Fanger and said, "Y'all sure you built this thang?"

I clenched my jaw, rolled my eyes and grabbed Fanger's left arm with my right hand to stop him from whoopin' Jack's ass.

Jack shrugged, dropped his head back down and turned his attention back to Peen-Iz.

Me and Fanger cracked open a couple of beers, expecting Peen-Iz to take for damn ever. But soon as I took my first swoller the ship hummed and bounced under my feet. My space reflexes was improving ever second I spent on one of them ships, and instinctively I spread my legs a little wider and bent my knees to keep my balance. The hum turned to a high pitched screech and I hollered, "This shit normal, Penis?"

Peen-Iz ignored my question and kept working the controls.

"Look at that shit," Fanger hollered, nudging my right arm with his left elbow.

I leaned forward slightly and stretched my neck towards the TV screen. A faint beam of light extended out in front of the ship several hundred feet kinda like headlights on a pitch black road. The light beam pulsed for a few seconds then spun around the ship like one of them lines on a radar screen. After several spins the light ray turned into a flat disc of light that surrounded the ship. Then the screeching stopped and ever thang went silent.

"That disc is the focused vibration waves from the shields," I heard Peen-Iz say to Jack.

The ship juddered and jerked and the asteroids grew larger on the TV screen. One of the bigger asteroids centered on the screen as Peen-Iz navigated directly towards it. The second the very edge of the light disc touched the asteroid the damn thang vaporized in to space. No explosion or nothing. Just a puff of gas or some shit and it was gone.

"It works," I mumbled.

"Damn straight," Fanger mumbled back.

My ears tingled, the ship jiggled a little and we took off into the asteroids, vaporizing ever one of the big ass space rocks the vibration disc touched. Not a damn thang happened to the ship. We flew straight on without even the slightest bump or jolt from impact.

Peen-Iz said something to Jack I couldn't make out and the ship dropped to a dead stop.

"What's happenin'?" me and Fanger said at the same time.

Peen-Iz ignored the question again and worked the controls. The ship hummed and bounced and the screeching started back up. The flat disc of light bulged up at the part closest to the ship and the swelling moved out to the edge of the disc like the way air fills one of them skinny balloons clowns use to make balloon animals. The high pitched screeching shifted to a low pitched creek, the ship bobbled from the left to right and the flat disc of light inflated completely to form a bubble around the entire ship.

The ship wobbled back in to motion as the creek grew louder and louder. We coasted through the asteroids, vaporizing ever damn one the bubble touched. The ship yawned one more long, giant creek then ever thang went silent again.

I didn't move for shit, my eyes locked on the TV screen. After just a second, a sucking kinda of implosion sound made my ears pop and the vibration bubble burst in to glittery little particles that dissolved away into space.

Peen-Iz danced his fangers over the controls, the ship stopped moving, and without looking up he said, "We blew out the shields."

"Just like all the speakers." Fanger tilted his head back, finished off his beer and shock his head.

"How the Hell did you know how to use the whoop ass device?" My gut was telling me Peen-Iz was somehow familiar with the technology but I wasn't completely sure.

"I didn't." Peen-Iz looked up at me with the blankest look I ever seen on that sumbitches face. "I just tinkered with the settings and that's what happened."

I turned to Fanger. The two of us was masters at reading each other's faces. We was both thanking it wasn't worth pushing back on Peen-Iz just yet. Not since he was still helping us. Or at least giving the impression he was helping.

"So now what?" Jack asked, snapping ever body back in to the moment. "Can we fix the shields?"

"We need stronger shields," Fanger said, nodding over at Peen-Iz. Fanger knew all about that sciencey shit.

Peen-Iz clapped his hands and said, "I know what to do."

"Well of course you do. That's convenient as shit," I muttered under my breath. I cracked open a beer, squeezed the can tight like I wanted to do to Peen-Iz's neck and stopped myself from completely laying in to that asshole. I kept reminded myself in my head right then wasn't the time. Ever bone in my body told me he knew much more than he let on, but pissing him off wasn't gonna do no good. I had to save the tongue lashing and ass whoopin' for later.

Peen-Iz twisted his mouth around a couple times, clearly holding something back. Then unexpectedly he shifted in to talky mode. "The whoop ass device is only as powerful as the shield generator, or any other vibration source, it's connected to. With a big enough vibration source I bet it could take out a whole planet. Matter of fact, with a big enough vibration source it could prolly take out whole solar systems. Our best option, since we need to be mobile and all, is a ship's shield generator. I know where we can get a ship with the strongest shield generator I ever seen."

"Where?" Me, Fanger and Jack said at the same time.

"Bom'Kyn," Peen said, and before any of us could say shit he kept talking. "We need to steal a clone ship."

I chugged a swoller of beer, Fanger grunted and Jack looked around at ever body with a blank ass look on his face. Going back to Bom'Kyn was risky as hell. For all we knew Peen-Iz had been working for the bigguns all along and all the shit that led up to this point was part of his plan to deliver us right in to their hands.

"Penis," I said with an angry chuckle, locking eyes with Peen-Iz. "I'm gonna need a minute with Fanger and Jack before we head off to Bom'Kyn."

Peen-Iz raised his right hand in the air and bobbed his head, keeping his eyes locked on mine.

Me, Fanger and Jack marched to the other side of the ship and huddled up.

"Well, fellers," I said, keeping one eye on Peen-Iz, "this here's one of them condundrooms."

"Yep." Fanger and Jack both nodded in agreement.

"Do we foller Penis to Bom'Kyn and execute his plan?" I took my eyes off Peen-Iz for a split second to look at Fanger and Jack. "Or do we go out on our own?"

"I don't know what we can do without Penis." Jack looked back over his shoulder at Peen-Iz. "Even if we get our hands on better shields or speakers or whatever I'm not sure we can connect the device and make it work."

"We can't trust his stankin' ass but I thank we ain't got no choice," Fanger said.

"A'ight then, guess we're going to Bom'Kyn," I said.

The three of us straightened up out of the huddle and drifted back over to Peen-Iz. This here situation was putting all of mine a Fanger's training to the test. We trained for the unexpected and this here was about as unexpected as we could get. What else could we do, really? We had to follow Peen-Iz back into the belly of the beast. We damn sure didn't stand a chance on our own trying to run them assholes off our planet. All we could do was keep moving forward and take ever challenge one step at a time. That's how we trained. And our training had kept us alive up till then so I figured it oughta keep on keeping us alive.

"So what's the plan, Penis?" I said, cracking open another beer. Dranking was always part of the plan.

"We need a clone ship," Peen-Iz said with a shrug. That's all he said. No long-winded explanation or nothing.

Me, Fanger and Jack stared at Peen-Iz and waited for more talking but he didn't say shit.

"You're gonna have explain why." I raised my eye brows real big.

"The DNA donors, like y'alls two friends, live in The Tower but that ain't where they make the clones." Peen-Iz shifted back in to talky mode. "It's gonna take a minute to explain."

Peen-Iz launched in to a windy ass tale about DNA donors, clones and the cloning process, exploding space ships and the bigguns only knowing some of what they needed to know to actually create clones. The point of it all was that the cloning process was dangerous as shit. Turns out the Bom'Kynians blow up more brand new clones than they actually use on missions. That's mostly because they stole the technology and never had any real training on how to use it. To make up for their ignorance, the Bom'Kynians devised an elaborate process of their own to protect themselves, to preserve as many DNA donors as possible and to create useable clones.

Me, Fanger and Jack drank three beers each and finished off one jar of moonshine listening to Peen-Iz's overly detailed description of the cloning process. I caught enough to extract the particulars of why the clone ship needs super strong shields. Basically, the clone machines are volatile and regularly explode with nuclear level destruction, and the majority of clones they successfully produce can't be controlled. The strong ass shields contain the nuclear explosions or, if needed, trap the savage, untamed clones long enough for the bigguns to self-destruct the ship themselves. For an extra level of protection the entire process is done in deep space far away from Bom'Kyn.

Peen-Iz went on and on and finally explained one more tidbit we needed to know. The two-man crew and the two DNA donors, that's the limit for every clone ship, have to actually be on the clone ship for the process to work. The two crew members have to guide, and depending on the level of coopera-tion, sometimes force the DNA donors in to the cloning machines. The bigguns experimented with the crew running the ships remotely but certain species of aliens just couldn't follow instructions for shit and others couldn't be sufficiently coerced from a distance. The brainwashing generally kept the DNA donors happy enough for them to cooperate but from time to time the crew members had to freeze up the DNA donors with a freezey gun to get them in the machine. When shit went wrong the crew and the DNA donors sometimes escaped the explosions or crazy ass clones in evacuation pods and sometimes they went down with the ship.

Our plan, which we all agreed to call Gammer Gammer Clone Grabber Zero Zero One, was to highjack the clone ship once it got out into deep space and before the cloning process starts.

According to Peen-Iz, if we got control of the ship quickly enough he could make it look like the ship exploded to the bigguns and they would never miss it.

"Fellers?" Peen-Iz slapped the top of the control panel with his right hand and tilted his head to the left. "Fellers? Y'all sure you understand the plan?"

"Yep," Fanger said.

"I think so," Jack shook his head and blinked his eyes real fast.

"Let's just do this shit." My head was still spinning from trying to pay attention.

"A'ight," Peen-Iz said, looking down at the control panel. "Jack, get over her and man the controls."

Jack stumbled in a zig zag pattern, leaned to the right and reached out his right arm to brace himself on the control panel. He tilted slightly back towards the left and stumbled in an arc, hanging on to the top of the control panel and letting his lanky right arm swang him in to position next to Peen-Iz.

Peen-Iz completely disregarded Jack's condition and asked, "We still invisible, Jack?"

Jacks head swayed in a circle as he tapped on the panel. "Yep, still invisible."

"Good," Peen-Iz said. "Take us back to Bom'Kyn and orbit the planet."

"Ten four," Jack said through a burp.

Me and Fanger both snickered a little. No matter the situation, talking through a burp was always funny. Then my ears tingled, I blinked and the next thing I knew Bom'Kyn popped up on the TV screen.

Somewhere during his long ass speech about the cloning process Peen-Iz turned himself in to Professor Peen-Iz. "Let's go over the plan," he said, crossing his right arm over his belly, resting his left elbow on his right hand and tapping his beard-covered chin with his left pointy fanger. "Lick, how do we find a clone ship?"

"It's easy as shit." I straightened my back and popped open a beer. "Clone ships take off from the planet ever few minutes and orbit the planet until they get the all clear from mission control to shoot out to deep space."

"Good." Peen-Iz gave me nod. "Fanger, how do we follow the ship in to deep space?"

"We stay invisible, hug up real close to the ship and latch on to it right before it goes in to hyper speed." Fanger took surprisingly well to Peen-Iz grilling us on the plan.

"Exactly," Peen-Iz said. He turned his head to

left, looked Jack up and down and said, "Open the weapons room, Jack."

Jack, despite his level of intoxication, responded to Peen-Iz's order with out hesitation, tapped the controls and the back wall of the ship swirled.

"Lick and Fanger," Peen-Iz said in a real soft voice, clearly trying to avoid sounding like he was given orders. "Y'all go get four freeze weapons, please. I need to show Jack how to latch on to the clone ship."

Me and Fanger looked at each other for a second then hustled off to the weapons room. We was getting good as shit at identifying the different devices on the ship and we both spotted the freezey thangs right away.

"When you figure Peen-Iz is gonna stab us in the back?" I said in a low voice as I grabbed one freeze weapon off the shelf with my right hand. I tapped my left hip with my left hand, making sure I still had the my freezey thang ready to go.

"I woulda figured right now woulda been the right time." Fanger reached his right hand for two more freezey thangs on the shelf and looked back over his left shoulder at Jack and Peen-Iz. "No tellin' what that asshole is up to."

"Maybe he ain't workin' for the bigguns," I said.

"Maybe not." Fanger hooked one of them freezey weapons on his left hip.

"You fellers, ready?" Peen-Iz hollered.

"Damn straight!" Me and Fanger hollered back. We jogged side by side back over to the control panel.

I turned my attention to the TV screen and said, "Dadgum, we're close as shit to that ship ain't we?"

"Get ready, Jack," Peen-Iz said, staring at the control panel. "Now!"

My ears tingled even more than usual, I got a wrenching in my belly I ain't never felt before, and the image on the TV screen turned to complete blackness. Then ever thang just stopped except for the blackness on the TV.

"Deep space," Fanger said, taking a swig from his whiskey bottle.

"We only got a few minutes," Peen-Iz said, "Where are the freeze weapons?"

I paused for a second. Giving Peen-Iz a freeze weapon coulda been a mistake. But we had to follow his lead. I lowered my right hand down to my leg and lobbed the freezey thang to Peen-Iz.

Peen-Iz opened his left hand, the weapon fell in to his palm and he smiled a big shit eating grin. He twitched his left wrist, the freezey thang spun around in his hand like he was gunslinger and then he hooked the damn thang through a loop on the left hip of his overalls.

Fanger slapped a freezey thang in to Jack's right hand, knowing better than to expect Jack to catch anything, and the four of us moved to the middle of the ship and circled up.

"Freezin' the crew is more important than freezin' the DNA donors." Peen-Iz fidgeted with some kind of remote in his right hand. "But we still gotta freeze'em all up."

Me, Fanger and Jack all nodded.

"Three. Two. One." Peen-Iz pushed a button on the remote with his right thumb.

Next thang I knew we was all standing on the bridge of the clone ship.

Peen-Iz extended his left arm, fired his freeze weapon and froze up the first crewman. Before any of us could react, he snatched the freezey thang outa Jacks hand with his right hand, pointed it and froze up the other crewman before that sumbitch sounded the alarm. Peen-Iz stood there, arms stretched out in a V shape, freeze weapons in both hands and two motionless crewmen floating in the air right in front of him.

"What the hell are you fellers waiting for?" Peen-Iz hollered.

I swiveled my head and twisted around, still getting reoriented from the transport over and not real sure what I was even looking for. Then I spotted them. The two DNA donors standing in one corner of the bridge. One was wearing a pink Polo-type shirt, green shorts and some kinda bulky brown shoes. The other wore a blue Polo-type shirt, khaki colored shorts and some kinda brown sandal thangs. Both of them had big ass heads with shaggy ass blond hair hanging down over their eyes.

"Hot dammit! They're Ralf'Lorians!Now freeze their asses!" Peen-Iz hollered.

Them DNA fellers just stood there not doing shit. Me and Fanger raised our right arms at the same time, mashed the button on our freeze weapons with our thumbs and froze up them sumbitches.

Peen-Iz side stepped, arms still in a V, and handed the freezey weapon in his left hand to me and the one in his right to Fanger. He hauled ass to a bunch controls on the back wall and started tapping, swiping, flipping switches and mashing buttons. After a few seconds he looked back and said, "We did it. We have the ship. The bigguns thank it blew up. We're in the clear."

I scrunched up my eyebrows and looked at Fanger and Jack. They looked back at me with their eyebrows scrunched up too. Gammer Gammer Clone Grabber Zero Zero One seemed like the easiest mission in the history of missions. Almost too easy.

WHOOPIN' ASS_

ME, Fanger and Jack just accepted how easy the acquisition mission went without over thinking it. We already knew we couldn't trust Peen-Iz for shit so we just got straight to prepping our new ship for battle. Peen-Iz transferred all of our supplies, all of the weapons and all of the light suits from the patrol ship to the clone ship with the transporter. We even transported the froze up patrol ship crew to one of the empty rooms.

Thangs was happening so easy I kinda started to forget a little that Peen-Iz was prolly gonna stab us in the back at any minute. Fanger was starting to relax some too. I'm purty sure I saw him and Peen-Iz chuckle together at one of Jack's farts. But I wasn't too concerned about either one of us slipping up. Me and Fanger was both good as shit at holding grudges.

Once we used the transporter for ever thing we could, Fanger, Jack and Peen-Iz headed back to the patrol ship to disconnect the invisibility device and whoop ass device manually. I manned the clone ship to keep an eye on the two crew sumbitches and the two DNA donors. We kept all four of them froze up in the corner of the bridge. While I waited I sipped a beer and explored our new vessel.

The clone ship was an older model ship than the rest we'd seen. No swirly walls. No bubbles and no farting through walls. Just real rooms, real hallways and real corridors. Except it did have that same fresh ass air like the other Bom'Kynian ships. Peen-Iz said the bigguns repurposed older ships to serve as clone ships. They figured most of them was gonna get blowed up so they didn't want to waist the newer models. Them buncha dumb, stankin', worthless asshole sumbitches had some sense, I reckoned. But still, ever damn thang I witnessed from mechanical equipment to computer terminals stretched way beyond any technology I ever saw.

I roamed around for a few minutes and made it all the way to the back of the ship. The bigguns stripped down most of rooms to bare walls, ceilings and floors so there weren't really much to see. Ever thang the crew needed, including the escape pods, was right up close to the bridge.

All in all, I kinda liked the bridge layout. It was a lot like the space ship bridges I saw in TV shows. Two captain's chairs sat dead center looking at a giant ass TV screen that completely covered the front wall. Behind the captain's chairs, all along the back wall from floor to ceiling were the controls. Sections of the back wall kinda spun around like the wheel on Price Is Right so short fellers could get to all the controls. Our patrol ship may have had newer technology but I felt more at home for some reason on the clone ship than any of the others we'd been on.

The cloning machine was right on the bridge against the wall to the right of the big ass TV screen. The damn thang didn't look nearly as complex as I expected and it was hard to believe it was destructive as shit by looking at it. It kinda reminded me of a big wood chipper truck. Peen-Iz said the DNA donors go in one side and the clones was spit out the other. After it was all done the DNA donors walk back out of the machine and the clones, if they could be controlled, was transported and stored in all the empty rooms of the ship.

I took the last swig of my beer and plopped down in the caption's chair that sat on the right when you was watching TV. Soon as I got settled the other fellers transported on to the bridge. Fanger sat down on my left and Peen-Iz and Jack went to work hooking up the devices to the main control panel on the back wall. Me and Fanger shared a jar of moonshine and twisted around in our chairs to watch Peen-Iz and Jack do the connecting.

The invisibility device, which Peen-Iz covered in some kinda black cloth, linked up without a hitch, but it took Peen-Iz a little longer to rig the whoop ass device. His ability to effortlessly make the necessary tweaks to connect the ship and the whoop ass device did even more to confirm my suspicions he knew more about the whoop ass device technology than he was saying. But all we needed for the time being was for all that shit to work right. Analyzing Peen-Iz would have to wait for later.

"We're all set to go. We need to test this shit before we head in to battle." Peen-Iz said, wiping his hands on the bib of his grungy overalls. None of us was so relaxed that we let Peen-Iz wear a light suit like me, Fanger and Jack. Peen-Iz whined and rambled on with some bullshit for a while, trying to convince us he needed a light suit, but finally he let it go.

"Initiating test." Jack mashed a button on the wall with his left pointy fanger. "We're invisible."

Peen-Iz grinned ear to ear, spun around on his heels and tapped out a code with his right fangers on a key pad that poked out half way up the back wall and just to the left of Jack.

Me and Fanger rotated around, settled in our chairs and watched the big ass TV screen in front of us. The ship trembled for a split second, the TV screen flashed and ever thang looked a little bluer on the screen than before.

"Whoop ass vibration bubble all set to go," Pee-Iz said.

"Take out the patrol ship." I pointed at the TV screen with all four fangers on my right hand. We all agreed with Peen-Iz that our patrol ship had to be vaporized to cover our tracks.

The patrol ship grew larger on the screen and then disappeared without even the slightest puff of gas. And our new ship didn't creak or moan or groan or nothing. Peen-Iz was right as hell. The clone ship shields combined with the whoop ass device worked perfectly together. The shit the whoop ass vibration bubble touched got gone easy peasy without the device putting any extra strain our our high powered shields.

"Time to run them sumbitches off our planet," Fanger said, wiggling up straight in his captain's chair.

"Take us to Earth, Jack," I said. "Let's initiate Operation Whoop Ass." We all decided to keep the name of this mission simple.

The sound of Jack tapping drifted past my ears, a slight tugging pulled in my belly and the TV screen went black. After a second the tugging stopped and the TV flashed back on again. On the screen I could barely see the blue and green of Earth through all the ships in orbit.

"What's the plan, Peen-Iz?" I twisted to the right in my seat and looked back over my right shoulder.

"Take out as many ships in orbit as we can," Peen-Iz said. "They have the most fire power. The ships in the atmosphere are science ships. They have minimal defensive weapons and ain't worth a shit in a fight. There's a command ship hidin' somewhere in the solar system. It ain't invisible but it can hide from sensors and shit. We need to draw that sumbitch out and destroy it before it blows up your planet."

I dropped back in my seat and looked to my left at Fanger. We both lurched forward, sprang out of our seats and spun right on our right heels to look at Peen-Iz.

"What the hell do you mean blow up our planet?" I scrunched up my eyebrows so tight it made my head hurt.

"Hot damn," Fanger mumbled, crossing his arms and locking his eyes on Peen-Iz. Them two wasn't going be chuckling together again any time soon.

"If the inhabitants fight back too hard the bigguns just blow up the planet. That's how they do it these days. They got enough wars goin' with other planets. They don't need another one." Peen-Iz looked at me and Fanger like we was the idiots.

"Why are you just now tellin' us this?" Jack said in a voice that sounded like Peen-Iz just took his puppy or some shit.

"We never made it this far before." Peen-Iz pulled on his long beard with both hands and his mouth dangled open. He was really confused by our reaction.

"Ok, so wait," I said, rubbing my temples with my pointy fangers. "What happens after we destroy the command ship?"

"They'll send another one to blow up Earth." Peen-Iz must have read our faces and knew he had to keep talking. "They'll keep sendin'em and we'll keep destroyin'em. I figure they'll give up at some point and just go away."

"That's the plan? Just hope they give up and go away," I said. "You ever seen the bigguns do that before?"

"Nope." Peen-Iz crossed his arms and rocked forward on the balls of his feet. "But I ain't never seen no inhabitants fighting all alone take out more than two command ships. The third command ship usually blows up the planet."

"Hot ole mighty." I squeezed my right hand so tight I damn near cracked the jar of moonshine I was holding. I didn't have a damn clue what to say at that point.

"Reckon we gotta make it past three command ships to see what happens." Fanger lifted the jar of moonshine outa my hand with his right hand, pokey fanger out.

I took in a deep breath of the fresh ass air. Fanger was right. Keep moving forward. That's how we always trained. We couldn't waist no more time. I exhaled, turned on my left heel, faced the screen and said, "Jack, vaporize these assholes."

"Ten-four!" Jack hollered.

I heard a switch flip and a button click. The image on the TV turned bluer, a whistley sorta whizzing sound rang out and everything on the screen turned to a blueish blur. I hollered, "What the hell am I seeing?

"Where circlin' Earth in hyper speed," Jack hollered. "I'm flying in a pattern kinda like rolling up a ball of yarn. We're taking out them assholes as we go."

"Hot damn! How many so far?" I glanced to my left at Fanger and he was grinning ear to ear.

"Twenty. Thirty-five. Forty. Hard to keep up with the sensor readings." Peen-Iz hollered. "Command ship comin' in to orbit. Jack, position us between the command ship and the planet and get ready to fly straight in to that sumbitch."

"Roger that!" Jack hollered.

The whistley whizzing faded out and the image on the TV screen stopped blurring. A big ass double decker flying saucer that reminded me of a Big Mac sat looking right back at us, jiggling faster and faster and glowing brighter and brighter red.

"They're powering up their weapon. Take'em out now, Jack!" Peen-Iz hollered.

The tug in my belly tugged harder than ever before and a slow rumbling sound kinda like thunder boomed louder and louder. The command ship grew bigger on the screen and then ever thang just stopped. And I mean ever thang. All sounds stopped. All the lights on the ship, all the controls and the TV screen. It all cut off. We was standing in pitch black and dead silence.

"Dude, what the hell, bro?" a voice echoed through the darkness.

The lights, the controls and the TV all flickered back on. The command ship was nowhere on the screen. The two Ralf'Lorians wandered out of the corner where they was froze up and the two crew sumbitches had their thumbs in their light suit straps.

"Dude, I straight up couldn't move, bro," the Ralf'Lorian in the pink shirt said.

"Bro, me neither, dude," the Ralf'Lorian in in blue said, raising his right hand to the other one for a high five.

"Peen-Iz you asshole!" one of the crewmen hollered.

Both the crew fellers grunted out angry grunts, straightened their arms and pulled their straps, activating their light suits.

Me and Fanger let our natural reflexes take control. Our thumbs shot through our light suit straps and we pulled in unison. We both leaned forward, shot our arms up in front of us and fired off the floor like rockets.

Them crew punks flew for the exit door off the bridge. They was fast but me and Fanger was faster. We soared over the top of them assholes, stretched our arms out the the side, spread our legs in a scissors kick and flipped forward. Our feet rotated over our heads and we twirled our bodies around to face them sumbitches like we was in the Matrix. We lined ourselves up directly between the crewman and the door.

Them two assholes tried to zig and zag but that didn't do shit. Me and Fanger seen better moves on the football field in high school. I reached in right my pocket with my right hand, pulled out my pocket knife and flipped the blade open with my thumb. My left hand instinctively drew the freezey thang off my left hip, and I looked to my right at Fanger. Me and him was both hovering in the air with our knives and freezey weapons set to go.

One crewman maneuvered low to go under us and one steered high to go over the us. Fanger bent his knees and pivoted his hips and shoulders to square himself up with the high feller. I leaned forward and kicked my feet back slightly to intercept the low feller. Them two dumbasses didn't change up nothing. They juked left and right but that didn't trick us for shit.

Fanger shot up and I shot down head first, aiming for the low feller. Right as that sucker flew under me, I tucked my knees, rotated my hips under my shoulders and dropkicked that sumbitch directly in his shoulder blades. That asshole bounced off the floor like a rubber ball and rebounded right up in front of me.

I smiled real big right in his stunned face, swung my right hand forward, and laced my blade between his light suit strap and chest. I flicked my wrist and pulled, slashing clean through the strap, and that asshole dropped to the floor. Automatically my left hand pointed the freezey weapon down between my legs. I mashed the button with my thumb, froze that sumbitch and then tilted my head up. Fanger had the other crew feller froze up too.

"What took you so long?" Fanger said with a grin. I thank finally getting to whoop some ass was lifting his spirits.

With the crewmen in tow, me and Fanger flew back to the corner on the left side of the TV where we had them froze up before. As we approached the corner my eyes darted around and I said, "Where are them DNA fellers?"

"Shit if I know," Jack said all fast and jittery, tapping like hell on the control wall. "Can't do shit about it. Gotta make sure we're invisible and the whoop ass device works."

"Ralf'Lorians are sneaky suckers," Peen-Iz said. "They can slink outa anywhere without being seen."

I scanned the bridge and didn't seem them fellers no where. I repositioned the crewman and said, "What the hell happened?"

"The command ship fired right before the whoop ass bubble made contact." Peen-Iz stared at the sensor readings. "We took a hit but the whoop ass bubble absorbed the force of the weapon and destroyed the command ship. When that shit happened it looks like some kinda electro waves passed through the bubble and blacked out ever thang electrical."

"I thank we're back to normal now." Jack glanced back at me and Fanger.

"Dude, this shit rocks, bro," a faint voice drifted in from around the exit door.

A second later them two Ralf'Lorians stumbled on to the bridge each with an empty jar of moonshine in their right hand and a half empty jar in their left. Soon as they was through the doorway they both bent their left arms, kicked their heads back and chugged what was left of the shine.

"Let's party!" the one in pink hollered. He lifted

both hands over his head and slammed the empty jars to the floor, shattering them to pieces. Then he leaned forward, stretched his arms out to the side and ran around like he was playing airplane. Just as that sumbitch got close to the clone machine his right foot hooked on his left heel and he tripped forward, stumbling directly into the clone machine. The automatic door closed behind him, red and blue lights I never even noticed before blinked, lighting the damn thang up like the Fourth of July, and the machine beeped a slow steady beep.

"Oh shit." Peen-Iz grabbed his beard with both hands and stared at the clone machine.

The beep stopped, the blinking red and blue lights changed to steady green lights and an electronic twittery sound emitted from the innards of the machine. A second later something that looked like a giant pink donut popped out of the back of the machine and rolled across the floor. When it reached the TV screen it spun around real slow a couple times then stopped. I got a good clear view of all sides of the thang and it weren't not giant donut. It was a giant rolling two sided butthole.

"Dudes," the Ralf'Lorian in blue stumbled in to the clone machine. "Where's my bro?"

The giant two sided butthole rolled up right

beside him, quivered real fast and sucked that sumbitch right into its sphincter hole. A second later, the rolling butthole convulsed and crapped out the nasties diarrhea I ever seen.

"Holy. Lee. Shit." Fanger waved his right hand in front of his face, pokey fanger out. "That giant butthole just shit him out."

The clone machine shot out another giant two sided rolling butthole and then another. The first butthole took position in the middle of the bridge in front of the TV and the other two rolled up in to formation on both sides of it. They all three spun around real fast like spinning tops then stopped with their front butthole sides facing all of us.

"Get ready, fellers," Peen-Iz said, shifting his eyes between me and Fanger and the control wall. "The first clones come out slow but the machine's gonna speed up and start spitting them suckers out."

"Laser guns!" I hollered.

The two captain's chairs on the bridge was equipped with laser guns to give the crew a fighting chance to make it to the escape pods if the clones went crazy. Me and Fanger never got time to test them lasers out but there ain't a gun in the universe me and him can't shoot. We both leaned forward, lifted off the floor and glided up next to our captain's chairs. We hooked our thumbs in our straps, pulled to cut off our light suits, landed on the floor and reached our right hands around our chairs.

My right fangers wrapped around the stock of the laser, I heaved and stumbled back. That damn laser gun was light as shit. I bent my right arm and bounced it up and down for a second to get the feel of it. If I didn't know better I woulda swore that thang was an empty Super Soaker. I hooked my left thumb in my strap and reactivated my light suit.

"Light them assholes up," Fanger said, with his light suit activated and laser in his right hand.

Me and Fanger raised our weapons, looked down the barrels with our right eyes and took aim. Fanger squeezed his trigger first and the laser pew pewed off a shot that hit the the first giant butthole square in the middle. That sumbitch sizzled for a second then melted into a pile of black ooze. I squeezed my trigger and Fanger fired off another shot. I zapped the one on the right and Fanger nailed the one on the left. Both them sumbitches sizzled and melted, adding to the pile of black ooze.

The twittering in the clone machine tweeted louder and faster like a damn looney bird and the whole machine shook and damn near lifted off the floor.

"Green seventeen!" I hollered. That was code for a defensive strategy me and Fanger developed in our training. Fanger takes the high ground and snipes whatever needs sniping and I stay on the ground and execute whatever needs executing.

"Second command ship on the sensors," Peen-Iz hollered.

Fanger launched off the floor to the ceiling and I sailed over to the clone machine. Soon as my feet hit the floor I hooked my left thumb in my light suit straps and extended my right hand towards the clone machine door.

"Don't open that!" Peen-Iz hollered, "You gotta wait for the cycle to finish or the machine will explode."

"How many this thang gonna make" I hollered back, retracting my hand away from the door.

"Shit if I know." Peen-Iz turned back to the sensors. "Hundreds, prolly."

The clone machine stopped shaking and went silent.

"Here they come!" Peen-Iz hollered.

Giant rolling two sided buttholes shot out the back of the machine and rolled across the floor. I flew over the top of the machine, aimed my weapon down and opened fire on them sumbitches soon as they poured outa the machine. They was popping out so fast I couldn't hit all of them. The ones I missed Fanger zapped from above before they even got close the Jack, Peen-Iz and the control wall.

"The second command ship is glowing red!" Jack hollered.

"Vaporize that sumbitch," I shouted, glancing at the TV screen to see another double decker flying saucer flashing red.

"Here we go!" Jack yelled.

My belly tugged and the thunder sound rumbled again. My light suit blinked off, the tugging in belly shifted to my tummy in my throat, and I sank down a foot or so. But before I could even react my light flashed back on and I was floating again. Ever thang else was black and silent. The clone machine, the ship's controls and ever thang electric was cut off. Mine and Fanger's light suits gave off enough light to see that even the giant buttholes stopped rolling. A second later ever thang flickered back on, the second command ship was gone from the screen and the red and blue lights on the clone machine flashed again.

"Where's Peen-Iz?" Fanger said from the ceiling.

I opened and closed my fangers on my weapon and looked back at the control wall. Peen-Iz was no where in sight.

"Fellers," Jack said, leaning his head to left and looking at a little screen. "We ain't invisible no more. Whoop ass device and shields are down too."

"They ain't gonna blow us up," I said, looking between Fanger and Jack. "They want the whoop ass device."

A staticky sensation radiated through my body and a crackling clicked and clacked all around. Ever hair on my body stood straight up and green bolts of electricity stretched from wall to wall and ceiling to floor. Next thang I knew a shit ton of critters was standing on the mountain of black ooze dead center in the middle of the bridge. They was the clones we fought on Earth but different. Maybelle Turner naked vampars, Bill Cooper flyn' fart monsters, Maybelle Turner white skinned tongue lashers and werewolf pro rassler fellers.

Me and Fanger didn't hesitate for shit. Without having to say a word, we both changed up the plan to protect Jack while he worked the controls. Fanger darted down to the floor and I bolted across the bridge. We took position side by side with Jack to our backs and opened fire. Me and Fanger trained in the junkyard for a full on frontal assault. He blasted ever thang that attacked from up and down and I wasted any critter or clone that charged from left, right or center.

The Bill Cooper flyin' fart monsters ripped out farts and bopped their way towards us. The Maybelle Turner naked vampars swooped down from the ceiling. The tongue lashers whipped and wagged their tongues and the werewolf pro rassler fellers leaped, springboarded off the walls, threw knees and elbows and rolled over the floor. The whole time the giant rolling buttholes barreled towards us, sucking up any of them critters that got close and crapping them suckers out. It was literally one big ass shit show.

Green lightning bolts crackled all around again and more critters appeared. The lights on the clone machine turned steady green, the twittering went ape shit and the damn thang bounced and banged. Sure enough, more giant buttholes rolled out and spread around the bridge. Me and fanger squeezed our triggers tight and held our ground. I swiveled left and right and Fanger titled up and down. Them laser guns didn't have the least bit of recoil and handled easy as shit. Ever thang we blasted sizzled and melted in to black ooze.

"Third command ship on sensors," Peen-Iz said outa nowhere.

I glanced right and caught a glimpse of Peen-Iz hovering by the control wall in a shiny new light suit. I side stepped right to give Peen-Iz some cover. That asshole was up to something for sure but I couldn't deny we needed his help.

Me and Fanger stood strong but there was too many clones and critters. They flew, hopped, rolled and thrashed closer and closer. As I rotated right, sweeping sumbitches with my laser blast, a nasty ass tongue lashed past my face from the left. I jerked my weapon back in that direction and the critter's tongue whipped straight for me again. Just before my laser beam ray tagged that sucker, that sumbitch's tongue clipped the perimeter of my light suit glow ball. Its feet lifted off the floor, its arms and legs snapped back behind it and my light suit reeled that sumbitch in straight towards me. The critter's face, with its tongue stretched around its jaw and back behind its head, froze within inches of my face. My light suit flashed bright then that sumbitch catapulted back away from me and flew all the way across the bridge, smacking dead center on the TV screen and sliding down to the gunk on the floor.

"Third command ship in firing range," Peen-Iz said calm as shit.

Soon as Peen-Iz finished talking a werewolf pro

rassler pounced up against the wall to his left, kicked off with both feet, and looking back over its right shoulder, aimed its right elbow at Peen-Iz's head for an elbow drop. Peen-Iz didn't even look in that critters direction. He just kept his eyes on the control wall. The werewolf pro rassler's elbow nicked the edge of Peen-Iz's light suit glow, the light orb caved in, pulling that sumbitch in and scrunching it up into a little ball, then slingshot its ass up to the high ceiling. The critter dropped like a rock and slapped down with a slosh as it landed in the mixture of crap and black ooze.

No critter, no critter body part or rolling butthole even got close to Fanger. He worked that laser gun like he was born with it in his hands. I can whoop any human, alien or artificially created critter's ass for damn sure. But Fanger was next level. He was made for whooping ass in space.

"Command ship glowing read!" Jack hollered.

"The whoop ass device might be working," Peen-Iz said with a shrug.

"Guess we'll find out," I said, "Go, Jack, go!"

That same damn tugging pulled at my belly but there weren't no thundering rumble. Just a grinding like turning on the garbage disposal with a spoon or some shit down in it. My light suit blinked off and on and then silence and darkness. No critter or clone in the room moved an inch. Shit flickered and ever thang was back on and moving again. Me and Fanger opened fire, grilling them suckers in to black ooze.

"I did it fellers!" Jack jumped up and down. "I got control of them rolling butthole clones!"

"Hell, yeah!" me and Fanger hollered at the same time.

Jack tapped the controls and ever one of them giant rolling buttholes spun around fast a shit, convulsed, sucked up the nearest clone critter and shit it out. It weren't a purty sight to see but we got the backup we needed.

The battle on the bridge raged on and on. Me and Fanger kept blasting them critters, our light suits repelled what ever needed repelling, the bigguns transported more of them sumbitches over and the clone machine cranked out more clones. Jack nestled in behind me and Fanger, tapping away on the controls, and Peen-Iz kept his eyes on the sensors. The giant rolling assholes and clone critters fought like hell and the bridge filled up with crap and black ooze. Then shit went from bad to worse.

"Fourth command ship, fellers," Peen-Iz said. "Whoop ass device and shields are gone."

"What should I do, Lick?" Jack turned around, rubbing his hands together.

I looked back over my left shoulder and Fanger looked back over his right, our fangers still squeezing our laser gun triggers. Me, Fanger and Jack gave each other a nod. None of us had to say shit. We knew what had to fight to the death to save Earth. That's the kinda fellers we was.

"Fly in to them assholes, Jack" I said.

To my surprise Peen-Iz didn't say shit to try and stop us. He just turned his back to the control wall, crossed his arms and looked at the TV screen. Me and Fanger fired our weapons and watched the TV too. I swollered and squeezed my gut in, expecting the tugging in my belly to start, but nothing happened. Then the command ship exploded on the screen.

"That wasn't us," Jack said.

Peen-Iz dropped his arms and whipped around to face the control wall. He leaned in close to the sensors and said, "Ships. A shit ton of ships."

I squinted at the TV. Little exploding dots flared up all over the screen and balls of light streaked past like little comets or some shit.

"The ships are takin' out them buncha dumb, stankin', worthless asshole sumbitches," Peen-Iz said, pulling his beard with both hands. "And the science ships are evacuating."

Then, just like somebody flipped a switch, the Bill Cooper flyn' fart monsters and Maybelle Turner naked vampars dropped to the floor and the Maybelle Turner tongue lashers and werewolf pro rasslers froze in their tracks. Not a damn one of them critters the bigguns transported over moved for shit.

"I thank somebody's trying to call us." Jack swiped and tapped on a little keypad.

The big ass TV screen flickered and all I could see was scrambled purple lines.

"Hey, fellers," a garbled voice said.

I turned to my left and said to Fanger, "Is that who I thank it is?"

"Hell yeah it is." Fanger grinned the biggest grin I ever seen on his face.

The image unscrambled and went clear as shit.

"Hey fellers, y'all need a beer?" Pick stood next Rang-er on the the bridge of a ship. "We decided to come to y'all. We brought an ass load of space ships too."

"Good to have y'all." I raised my left arm and wiped a tiny drop of sweat off my forehead with my left wrist. "Damn good."

"Damn skippy." Fanger gave our double gangers a thumbs up with his right hand, pokey fanger out.

"Fellers," Jack said, turning in a circle and looking around. "Where's Peen-Iz?

Me and Fanger jerked our heads to the right and looked back over shoulders at the control wall.

"The invisibility device and whoop ass device are gone." I squeezed my laser gun tighter with both hands.

"That asshole." Fanger leaned to the right, lifted off the floor, rotated his hips and shoulder forward, and with his laser gun pointed in front of him, torpedoed for exit door.

I spun on the heel of my right foot, stepped my left forward, ran for a couple steps and dove in to the air. I cut a sharp right, passed through the door and Fanger, firing his laser, swerved left directly in front of me. I caught a quick glimpse of Peen-Iz hovering in the air, hugging the invisibility device and whoop ass device in his left arm and pointing some kinda gun with his right hand. Arcs of electricity crackled around me and a laser bolt landed square on my chest. I grabbed my chest with both hands, dropping my weapon, and sank to the the floor.

Through the flickering of my light suit I saw Fanger blasting Peen-Iz with his laser. That didn't do shit. Peen-Iz's light suit absorbed the impact. Fanger swerved right and another blast from Peen-Iz's gun barely missed the edge of his light suit glow. Fanger dropped his laser gun and rammed straight in to Peen-Iz.

My light suit buzzed, crackled and blinked off. I slammed hard on floor. My body ached from head to toe and tried to push myself up with both hands. I didn't have the strength. The laser beam zapped ever bit of energy I had in my body. I dropped back down on the floor, laid flat on my chest and belly and looked up towards Fanger and Peen-Iz. I thank I blacked out cause the next thang I saw was Fanger and Peen-Iz standing toe to toe with knives in their right hands, the left straps of both their light suits dangling in front and back and the two devices spread out on the floor.

"We don't gotta do this," Peen-Iz said, dancing side to side on his toes.

Fanger didn't say shit. Like I said, he don't talk and bullshit when he fights. He danced side to side, matching Peen-Iz's speed, shuffled his feet backwards then lunged forward.

Peen-Iz side stepped onto his left foot and Fanger stepped out wide with his right foot, realigning himself with Peen-Iz. Fanger's left hand latched on to Peen-Iz's right wrist and Peen-Iz's left hand snagged Fanger's right wrist. They slammed together chest to chest and each one twisted the knife out the others right hand.

Peen-Iz drove his left knee up fast as shit at Fanger's man junk. Fanger raised his right leg and twisted a little to his left, deflecting the force Peen-Iz's knee, then stomped his right foot and pushed Peen-Iz in the chest with both hands. Peen-Iz stumbled backwards, thrust his hips back, swung both his arms around in big circles and hopped backwards to regain his footing.

They stood toe to toe again, right feet back, left feet forward and fists up. At exactly the same time they both drove off their right leg, shifted their weight to the their left feet and threw right hooks that landed square on the others left jaw. Both them fellers staggered and teetered sideways, rubbing their left cheeks with their left hands and twisting their jaws. I swear neither one of them have ever been hit that hard by anybody else in their lives. They was both tough as shit and a damn near equal match up.

Peen-Iz backed away, putting distance between him and Fanger and said, "I would like to stay and whoop your ass but I ain't got time for this shit."

Fanger tucked his head, fired off like a rocket and charged at Peen-Iz like a rhino.

Peen-Iz stood his ground, reached his right arm behind his back, then slung his right hand back around holding a weapon I ain't never seen before. Right before Fanger wrapped his hands around that sumbitch's neck, Pee-Iz fired, blasting Fanger in the chest at point blank range.

Fanger twitched and trembled like he was being possessed by a demon, then snapped straight up stiff as a board and toppled over, slamming face down on the floor. Fanger don't give up for shit. He twisted and squirmed, grunted and growled, and slithered across the floor towards Peen-Iz.

"I told you fellers I was gonna help you free your planet. I never said I was gonna hang around after." Peen-Iz kicked the invisibility device, still wrapped in black cloth, and the whoop ass device in to the escape pod with his left foot while keeping his weapon aimed at Fanger.

"What the hell is your deal, Penis?" I said, struggling to talk. "You our friend? Our enemy? What?"

"I ain't nothing," Peen-Iz said. "I'm just gone."

Peen-Iz tilted to the right, ducked and stepped sideways to the right in to the escape pod. He turned around to face out, squat down and grinned at me and Fanger. The door hissed a slow hiss and lowered down to seal up the pod. Just as the sliding door passed his knees Peen-Iz hollered, "You sumbitches!"

The door suctioned closed and the pod ejected from the ship.

I wiggled on the floor and wrenched my neck back to see Jack floating in the air, holding a spot porter in his right hand and the invisibility device and whoop ass device on the floor under his feet.

"We trained you good," I mumbled then blacked out completely.

EPPER LOG_

Me and Fanger came full circle. We caused an alien invasion with one of our inventions and saved Earth using our training. But our planet ain't the same no more. A shit ton of people were taken to serve as DNA donors, all the damn mini golf courses ever where are driving the people left behind crazy, and now us and ever body else knows for a fact that aliens are real. All that shit combined made it easy for me, Fanger and Jack to make the decision to leave Earth and join the war against Bom'Kyn.

We kept possession of the clone ship, the invisibility device and whoop ass device. Jack swears he can get the devices working again and he's gonna teach me and Fanger how to operate the ship. We unfroze the patrol ship crew and clone ship crew and made deal with those fellers. If they cleaned all the giant rolling butthole crap and black ooze off the bridge we would drop them off on some kinda deserted planet somewhere. Them suckers jumped at the opportunity and cleaned the ship spic and span. Now we're all set to go in our very own space ship.

Joining the war is only part of our mission. We're searching for answers to some lingering questions. We came to realize Peen-Iz may have been right about the whoop ass device. Maybe me and Fanger didn't build that shit completely on our own. We wanna discover the origins of the device and how me and Fanger came in to possession of the technology. And, most importantly, were gonna track down Peen-Iz and whoop his ass. See y'all in space.

ALSO BY LICK DARSEY /
R.D.SMITH / ROB DOUGLAS_

Lick Darsey is a pen name for Rob Smith. Rob also writes
under the names R.D. Smith and Rob Douglas.

Dang: A Humorous Mystery

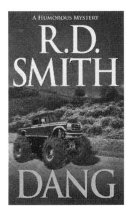

Ain't Weird Yet: Entry One

AIN'T
WEIRD YET

ENTRY ONE
ROB DOUGLAS

Thank you for reading!

If you liked *Lick and the Invasion*
please leave a review.

Me and Fanger would appreciate it.

Made in United States
Orlando, FL
19 October 2023

38012826R00148